DEATH RAFT

Frank scanned the sea with the binoculars. Joe wasn't among the men in the water, and Frank turned his gaze on the raft. He grinned with excitement.

Joe was standing up in the raft.

"It's Joe," Frank said happily.

Then there was a thunderous explosion.

When Frank looked through the binoculars again, the raft was a ball of fire, flying apart above the waves.

Books in The Hardy Boys™ Casefiles Series

THICK AS THIEVES

FRANKLIN W. DIXON

AN ARCHWAY PAPERBACK
Published by SIMON & SCHUSTER

New York   London   Toronto   Sydney   Tokyo   Singapore

An Archway paperback
first published in Great Britain
by Simon & Schuster Ltd in 1992
A Paramount Communications Company

Copyright © 1988 by Simon & Schuster Inc.

Simon & Schuster Ltd
West Garden Place
Kendal Street
London W2 2AQ

THE HARDY BOYS, AN ARCHWAY PAPERBACK
and colophon are registered trademarks of Simon & Schuster Inc.

THE HARDY BOYS CASEFILES is a trademark
of Simon & Schuster Inc.

Simon & Schuster of Australia Pty Ltd
Sydney

A CIP catalogue record for this book is
available from the British Library

ISBN 0-671-71619-0

Printed and bound in Great Britain by
HarperCollins Manufacturing, Glasgow

THICK AS THIEVES

Chapter

1

"Go away," said the thin man who stood between Frank Hardy and the single open entrance to the darkened Bayport Museum.

Caught off-guard, Frank took a step back and blinked in the harsh artificial light from overhead. The man in front of him folded his arms and smirked, almost begging Frank to try to push by.

Frank knew that look, from other bullies he'd run across. At first glance, this one didn't have the usual bully equipment—he was almost a head shorter than Frank, who stood just over six feet tall, and much older, with dark, thinning hair that had worked back on both sides into a widow's peak. His thick glasses magnified his eyes, making them look far too large for his head. An ill-fitting suit hid his physique. The man might have been athletic once, but had long since let himself go—a small potbelly spread out from under his thin chest. Frank had no doubt he could push past the guy without any effort.

But there was that smirk, the smug grin of a man who had a rule book behind him, if not muscle. It was the look of a clerk who could use the power of a large company—or government—to make himself feel big.

"Who does this guy think he is?" an angry voice burst out from the darkness behind Frank. It was his younger brother, Joe. He was seventeen, a year younger than Frank, with blond hair and a powerhouse build, in contrast to Frank's brown hair and lean frame. Joe's approach to problems was different from Frank's too.

"We're supposed to be here," Frank explained. "Chief Collig hired us to handle security for one of the museum exhibits."

"Who cares?" the man snapped back.

Joe moved into the light beside his brother, clenched his fists, and glared at the guy.

One look at Joe's angry, flashing blue eyes and the man's smug mask cracked. With a frightened gasp of breath, the guy stepped back, opening his hands in front of his chest to ward off any possible punches.

Frank put an arm out to hold Joe back. "Cool down," he said to his brother. Then he turned his attention back to the man and stared coldly into his eyes. "Mind telling me *why* we can't go in?"

The man returned his level gaze, his confidence returning. From his pocket he drew an ID card. "Elroy Renner, American Insurance Investigators. You're interfering with official business. Now move off."

Joe snatched the card from Renner, glanced at it, and grinned. "I guess you're here with the new exhibit."

Angrily Renner grabbed the card back and slid it into his pocket. "Listen, kid. I'm in charge of security around here, and if you know what's good for you—"

"Who's in charge?" a deep voice boomed from inside the museum. Chief of Police Ezra Collig stepped through the door, his face red with rage. "Renner! What have I told you?"

Renner glared at the chief, the two men locked in a duel of stares. "The insurance company left operations in my hands, not—"

"This is *my* town," Collig interrupted. "No one tells me what to do in my town. The insurance company sent you to work with me, not to run the show."

Renner's jaw dropped. "I'm not going to

leave the protection of valuable gems in the hands of some hick-town cop.''

"Hick town!'' Joe yelled, and Renner spun toward him. The thin man's eyes darted from Joe to Frank to Chief Collig, then back to Joe. Sourly rolling his eyes, he gave up the argument and slunk into the museum.

Collig chuckled. "He's a good man, really— but a real pain in the neck to work with sometimes.'' In a grand gesture, the chief swept his arm toward the open museum door and winked at the Hardys. "After you, boys.''

Frank drew a deep breath and looked up at the front of the building before entering. He always found the museum inspiring. An old mansion, it had four spires rising to the sky like corner towers on a castle. The spires were being rebuilt as part of a plan to renovate the museum. Scaffolding rose up around them, making the museum look like a castle under siege. The building was set back from the street and separated from other houses by woods and a huge lawn.

Inside, a short foyer opened into a parlor the size of a normal house. The walls were lined with heavy gold-framed paintings, and in the center of this main room was a giant sculpture of bronze and chrome. Frank wasn't exactly sure what it was supposed to be. The last time he'd been in the museum, a statue of a Greek warrior had stood there.

He remembered it well—the statue had fallen and almost killed Tessa Carpenter back in *The Borgia Dagger* case.

"Could use your help," he heard Chief Collig say as they left the room and walked down the carpeted hall. He realized Joe and the chief had been talking while he'd been deep in thought.

"I don't know," Joe was saying. "I thought the Bayport police didn't like working with us amateurs."

Collig smiled apologetically. "Sure, I prefer not having to look over my shoulder for you two whenever a crime happens in this town. But this is different. We need security guards to watch the Star of Ishtar exhibit. I don't have the manpower to staff a special detail like this twenty-four hours a day."

"I read about the exhibit in the paper," Frank said. "The Star is one of the largest sapphires in the world."

"Right. And I need people I can trust."

"You can trust these two?" Renner had reappeared almost magically and was leaning in a doorway, his arms tightly crossed.

"I'd rather trust them than all your electronic gadgets," Collig snapped back. "I've known these boys for years. They're smart, honest, and they've got great instincts."

"Electronics don't need instincts," Renner replied. He pushed open a door, and the four of them walked through it. The relatively dark space on the other side was large. It was a corner room, and one of the spires rose a hundred feet above it. The floor was a rich marble, and exhibit cases lined the brocaded walls. In the center, surrounded by electric eyes and vibration alarms, was an eight-sided glass case.

"There," Renner said proudly, "is the Star of Ishtar!"

Frank's eyes widened.

There was nothing in the case.

"It's empty," Joe said. For a moment Frank thought Renner was going to collapse like a balloon with the air let out. His face went chalk white, and his mouth flopped open, then shut without a word coming out.

Chief Collig stepped forward with his usual no-nonsense attitude and tested the defenses. When his fist passed through the electric-eye beam and pounded on the glass, alarms began to shriek.

"Well, that ought to bring reinforcements," Collig muttered, his eyes darting around the room.

"This is your fault!" Renner screamed.

"There was supposed to be someone in this room at all times!"

"There would have been!" Collig answered. "If you hadn't been playing drill sergeant and stopped the Hardys from coming in. I had to come find you to see what was taking so long."

"So you admit it!" Renner bellowed. "The loss is your responsibility."

"Let's worry about getting the stone back before we decide who's to blame," Frank suggested. "How could anyone manage to steal the Star without tripping the alarms?"

He studied the case, and then the room. Nothing seemed out of place. Puzzled, he glanced up into the darkness of the spire.

About sixteen feet up a flicker of motion caught his eye.

"A rope!" Frank cried. "Someone hit the lights. Joe, come here."

As Collig hit the switch that lit the spire, Joe reached his brother's side. "Get me up there," Frank said. Joe cupped his hands together, and in seconds Frank stepped from Joe's hands to his shoulders and was leaping for the rope.

It was just within his grasp. Quickly Frank started to work himself up hand over hand. As his eyes adjusted to the lights, he looked straight up.

Almost at the top of the spire, also climbing the rope, was a woman in a black jumpsuit.

When she glanced down at him, Frank saw she was young and beautiful, with reddish blond hair sweeping over her shoulders.

"I don't believe it," Joe said when he caught a glimpse of the woman's face. "It's Charity."

"Who's Charity?" said Collig, bewildered.

"Don't ask," Joe muttered, shaking his head. The beautiful young jewel thief had made a fool of him once. Could Frank even the score?

"Get outside and have the building surrounded," Frank called down. "I'll keep climbing. Let's give her nowhere to go." Already he could hear the sirens of reinforcements arriving outside. They had Charity trapped.

For what seemed an eternity, Frank continued to pull himself up. He was almost within reach of the woman dangling above him. She was peering out through a skylight at the top of the spire as if she were waiting for something or someone.

"Why, Frank Hardy," she said, finally deciding to acknowledge him. "I haven't seen you since when? San Francisco? Is your brother still as cute as ever?"

"Give it up, Charity." Frank's voice was gravelly from the exertion of the climb. "We've got you surrounded."

"That may be," Charity admitted, the lovely

smile never leaving her lips. Her hand slipped into her jumpsuit and came out a second later with a glint of silver.

Charity moved so fast, Frank hardly saw the knife as she slashed the rope.

Frank sucked in a last breath and pictured with horror the long plunge to the marble floor below.

Chapter

2

AFTER A COUPLE of inches Frank's fall stopped. The shock jarred the rope from his grasp. He desperately grabbed for it and tightened his grip around the heavy cord.

Swaying one-handed in midair, he was holding on for dear life.

After he had caught his breath, Frank looked up to see why he hadn't plunged all the way to the floor below. Charity hadn't cut the rope all the way through. A single strand had him dangling in the air. If he remained perfectly still, the strand might support his weight until help came. If he moved, the strain on the rope would snap it, and he would plummet to the hard floor.

But if he stayed where he was, Charity would escape, and Frank couldn't let that happen.

Slowly he eased himself up, putting as little strain on the strand as he could. The rope slipped another inch, and he froze to stop its swaying. After a moment he started working his way up again, but the strand kept untwining.

Frank knew he wouldn't make it.

From above he heard a metallic creaking, and looked up to see Charity opening one of the glass skylights at the top of the spire. A blast of cool night air gusted in, sending the rope swaying again. Another fiber popped loose from the strand.

Frank closed his eyes and took a deep breath. He had to make his move and get up past the raveled strand.

He gathered his strength. Then, in a flurry of movement, he pulled himself up in a couple of rough, rapid motions. The rope dropped by another inch. His hand was almost past the split when the last fibers pulled loose and the strand broke.

Frank lashed out, his fingertips grazing the top rope, but he couldn't get a grip on it. His fingers slid along the rough fibers, then closed on empty air.

No! They'd caught on the tail end of the frayed strand. Frank's fingernails dug into his palm as he clung to it. The pain in his fingers blotted out all thought. By instinct he threw his free hand up and caught hold of the rope. Ignoring the burning in his shoulders, Frank pulled himself the rest of the way to the window in the spire.

As he crawled out the window, the pain caught up to him, and Frank collapsed on the scaffolding. The cool air washed over him, and he opened his eyes to see what looked like a giant bat standing over him.

Frank shook the pain from his head and stared. It was no bat.

Charity smiled down sweetly at him and blew him a kiss. Before Frank could reach her, she leapt off the scaffolding. The wind caught the hang glider she had strapped herself into, and she was gone, a shrinking, winged dot vanishing into the dark.

A spotlight hit Frank, blinding him, and from the ground came a voice through a megaphone: "You're surrounded. Give yourself up." It was Elroy Renner. Frank yelled back and pointed to Charity, but they were too far away to hear him and in the wrong location to see Charity's flight. Frustrated, Frank began the long climb down the scaffolding.

"Where is she?" Chief Collig asked as Frank reached the ground.

"Gone," Frank said on the run. "She took

off in a hang glider." He had Joe by the arm now. "Come on."

"Wait!" Renner shouted. "You can't just run out! You have questions to answer!"

"Later," Frank shouted back as he and Joe raced to their black van in the museum parking lot. "When we catch Charity, we'll have all the answers."

"How are we going to catch her?" Joe asked, climbing into the passenger's seat. He yanked the seat belt around him. "If you lost sight of her, she could be anywhere."

The van had roared to life, and with a screech peeled out of the parking lot and onto the street. They headed for the west end of Bayport.

"She took off over the west woods," Frank said. "If she plans to make a safe landing—and there's no guarantee of that—there's only one place she can do it."

Joe snapped his fingers. "The old Miller farm. It's the only clear, flat land for miles."

"Right," replied Frank. "I can't wait to bring her in."

"You?" Joe said. "*I'm* the one she made a fool of in San Francisco."

"She did a pretty good job of that with both of us, brother."

Joe grinned. "That'd really be something, wouldn't it? Us capturing the greatest jewel thief of the decade—'' He stopped as the gates to the old Miller place appeared in the headlights.

The Miller farm had been one of the many in the Bayport area, but times had changed. Farmers had moved out, and more and more of their land had been built up with new housing developments. Yet, even as the city swallowed up so much land, this old farm remained untouched, even after the last Miller died. Now it was a slowly collapsing monument to a way of life that had all but vanished from that part of the country.

The lock that should have been on the gate wasn't there. Frank killed the headlights as Joe got out of the van and pulled open the barrier. The van rolled onto the farm.

"There's a light on at the house," Joe said. He stood on the step of the van, hanging out the open door. Something dark spread out across the road in front of them. "Watch it."

Frank brought the van to a stop. "Charity's hang glider," he said, getting out of the van. "If we run over that, it'll make so much noise that she'll know we're here. Let's leave the car and not move the glider. It'll be quieter approaching on foot."

Joe grinned. "I can't wait to see the look on her face when we burst in on her."

Quietly they crept through the tall weeds and

then across the grass to approach the house. The curtains were drawn, but a woman's shadow fell on them, moving back and forth. Frank squinted. There was something odd about the silhouette, but he couldn't put his finger on what.

"Let's hope she's alone," he said. "I'd hate to run into someone toting a gun."

Joe reached the house first and flattened his back against it. Inside, the shadow still walked back and forth. "If she's got the Star, she'll have already dumped any partner she might have had. Charity uses people, but she never splits the loot with them."

"Looks like she's waiting for someone," said Frank, who had flattened himself against the wall next to Joe. "Let's not disappoint her."

They reached the door. It was solid wood, but years of decay had splintered and weakened it. It gave slightly against Joe's testing shove.

"Ready?" he whispered. Frank nodded.

Joe threw down one finger, and then a second. On the third finger, the Hardys stepped away from the door, then hurled their shoulders into it.

The door cracked open with a sound like a sudden thunderclap. It fell away, and the Hardys rushed into the farmhouse. All the furniture was still there, covered with a thick layer of dust. There was no sign that anyone had lived there in recent months.

Frank didn't hang around to check out the decorating. They ran for the living-room door and rushed into the lit space.

In the middle of the living room was a lamp, trained on the window. Between the window and the light was a record player, its turntable moving round and round. Riding around was a cardboard cutout shaped like a woman's head and shoulders. The shadow cast by the light seemed to move back and forth across the curtains. Cords from both the light and the record player ran to a small portable generator in a corner of the room.

That was it—there was no sign of Charity.

"A trick!" Joe roared. "She's not here at all."

"What's that noise?" Frank cut across Joe's yelling. From somewhere came a low hum, like that of a giant electric fan that was growing louder and louder.

"Outside!" Joe dashed for the front door.

"I've got a bad feeling about this," Frank said, following on the heels of his brother. "Remember old man Miller, back when we were kids? How he used to entertain at fairs?"

"Barnstorming," Joe recalled. "He did flying tricks in an old biplane."

"And his barn is built to store a plane," Frank said, leading the way now, to the barn. "That's how she's going to get out of here! She has a plane stashed here."

They flung open the barn doors, and a blast of air hit them in the face. The single engine of a biplane roared in their ears. The boys rushed in, raising their arms to keep the blowing dust out of their eyes. They could just make out a woman sitting in the pilot's seat.

"Charity," Joe yelled, but his voice was drowned by the engine noise. There was a grinding of machinery behind him, and he turned—too late—to see the barn doors closing. There wasn't enough space for them to get out.

"Frank!" Joe shouted. "The doors!"

They rushed over and pressed their hands against the doors, struggling to keep them open, but strong motors forced them shut. Charity stuck a remote control out the side window, and on her lips she plastered a smile.

Bits of straw were sucked into the propeller and were shredded. As Frank and Joe pressed back against the barn door, the plane began to move forward.

The propeller, slicing everything in its way, was aimed straight at them.

Chapter
3

"SCRAMBLE," FRANK YELLED, diving to the ground to avoid the whirling blade. Joe rolled under a wing as the plane passed over him.

With a laugh, Charity aimed the remote control at the barn doors again and pressed a button. They swung wide open, and the plane rolled away from the Hardys and out into the night.

"Stop her!" Joe yelled. He leapt for the tail of the plane, which rolled along on a single wheel. He was too late. The biplane was already in the air.

Charity was out of reach.

"It figures she'd be able to fly a plane," Joe said, brushing himself off after his hard landing. "She's an expert at everything else. We'll never catch her."

"Maybe," Frank said, every bit as annoyed as Joe by the escape. "That doesn't mean we shouldn't try. She's obviously been using this place as her base of operations. Maybe she left something behind to trace her by." They went back to the house.

A search of the bedrooms and kitchen turned up nothing. Neither did a check of the record player.

As Joe moved the lamp that had shone on the window, a tiny scrap of paper fluttered out from under the bottom of it and settled near his shoe. He picked it up and studied it. It looked like a duplicate from an order form, with serial numbers on it.

"I think I found something," he called to Frank.

Frank walked over to Joe and took the paper from him. "I'd say it was a piece of a receipt. It looks vaguely familiar, but I'm not sure why or where it's from."

Joe sighed. "One thing I *am* sure about is that there's nothing else to find here. We'd better get back to town and give them the bad news."

The mood back at the museum was bleak. A line of police officers barricaded both ends of the street that the museum was on, keeping reporters and TV camera crews out. Frank and Joe were let through the barricade and shortly found themselves in the museum curator's office, where Chief Collig sat on a couch, with Officer Con Riley nearby, leaning against a wall. Both sets of eyes were on Renner. Renner was speaking on the phone, but he talked too quietly to be heard across the room. Though good friends, Collig and Riley didn't speak. Right then there was nothing to say.

Riley's eyes rolled up as the Hardys entered the room. Unlike Chief Collig, he had never minded the Hardys helping out on cases, but he also knew that wherever Frank and Joe were, trouble was sure to follow. "Your father know you're here, boys?"

The Hardys' father was Fenton Hardy, a former New York police detective who had become a world-famous private investigator. It wasn't unusual for him to take off across the globe at the drop of a hat—which Frank and Joe sometimes did as well.

"Mom and Dad are in Boston for the week," Joe said. "Dad recommended us for this security gig because he couldn't be here."

Riley grinned. "I suppose he thought it would be easy."

"Wipe that stupid grin off your face," Renner growled as he slammed the phone down.

He pointed to the chief. "I want this man arrested."

All four stared at Renner, stunned. Chief Collig bounced to his feet, angrily asking, "And what am I to be arrested for?"

"You stole the Star," Renner said, glaring at Collig. "You stole it while I was out front talking to these kids." He waved a hand in the direction of the Hardys. "Then they concocted this story about a jewel thief to cover your tracks."

"She was there!" Frank protested.

"Says you," Renner said bluntly. "I didn't see anyone. Suddenly you three were tripping alarms and pulling stunts, till I couldn't tell what was what. But the thief had to be someone who knew how to turn the alarms on and off and who could get to them. That means Collig or me. And I was with the boys."

"It was Charity," Joe said. "We have proof." He held up the scrap of paper. Renner snatched it, studied it for a moment, then crumpled it into a little ball and tossed it back to Joe.

"Stray garbage," the insurance man said. He pointed a finger at Collig again.

Con Riley glared at Renner, his hands on his hips. "There's no evidence against the chief, and he's too fine a man for you to accuse."

"I should have figured you hick-town cops

would stick together," Renner snarled back. "But I know what my report is going to say."

"If you think you've got something on me, do whatever you have to," Chief Collig said. "But don't you speak to my officers like that. And don't forget that I'm still chief of police in this town."

"You won't be much longer if I have anything to say about it," Renner said. "And I will. The insurance company I work for has lots of pull in this state. No yokel cop is going to make fools of them. Collig, you can kiss your job goodbye." He eyed the Hardys. "Now, what about these two?"

"They're free to go," Riley said.

"No, we're not free." Joe gave Renner a look so menacing the insurance guy jumped a step back. "We're going to find Charity, bring back the sapphire, and wreck this little frame you're trying to put around the chief and Frank and me."

"I've got it!" Frank cried. "Joe, where's that scrap of paper?"

As Joe handed him the numbers, Frank went behind the curator's desk and dug out a phone book. "Airlines, airlines . . ." he mumbled, running a finger down a column in the Yellow Pages. He picked up the phone and dialed a number.

"Hi," he said in a cheery voice. "I'm afraid

I've destroyed my plane ticket, and all I have left of it is the order number. I think it was with your company. Could you check? . . . Thank you." He rattled off the number on the paper.

"Oh. Transcontinent Air. . . . I see. Thank you. And that flight was to . . .? Sorry, but my appointment book was destroyed at the same time. I go so many places on business, I can't keep track of them. . . . Thanks.

"Of course. Thanks. And the flight is leaving . . . It just left. Oh, dear. Is there any other flight I can— When? . . . Tomorrow morning? That'd be great. Two tickets, please. . . . Hardy. . . . Yes. You've been very helpful."

Frank hung up the phone, cold determination on his face. "Let's go, Joe. We have some packing to do."

"Where do you think you're going?" Renner snapped.

"San Diego," Frank said, trailing Joe out of the room. They slammed the door behind them.

Joe Hardy woke the minute the plane touched down on the runway in San Diego. He and Frank both knew that that might be the last time they'd have to sleep in days. They had drifted off as soon as they left New York.

Joe almost wished he hadn't. His rest had been constantly interrupted by nightmares of Charity.

He nudged Frank awake. "I've been thinking—" he began, as the plane rolled up to the terminal, but Frank interrupted him.

"Me, too. Something's not right here." Frank yawned and stretched. "It strikes me that Charity could've escaped from us several times. Why was she so slow?"

"Slow?"

"Sure. First, she dangles on that rope until we see her, then she stays on the scaffolding outside until I get there."

Joe nodded. "And she was way ahead of us in the barn. She could have flown away before we got anywhere near her."

"But instead she closed the doors and played with us," Frank agreed. "Sounds a little like she was trying to make sure we stayed on her trail, doesn't it?"

"You think she left the number for us to find?"

"I don't know. There's only one way to find out."

"Right," Joe said. "Catch Charity." The flight attendants opened the doors, and the passengers started filing out of the plane. Trapped in their seats until the flood of people passed, Frank and Joe watched each of them move by. Finally, when the plane was almost empty, the Hardys got up.

"Here's something else that's funny." Joe lowered his voice. "I just recognized about half a dozen of the people on this plane."

"Me, too," Frank said, frowning. "We've seen their faces in those investigator's updates Dad gets. They're criminals."

"Thieves," Joe added. "Just like Charity. What are they all doing in San Diego at the same time?"

"Do criminals have conventions?" Frank asked jokingly. Then his face grew serious "Something's going on. The question is, what, and what are we going to do?"

They stepped into the terminal. Already the passengers were dispersing, but just ahead Joe saw a familiar hairless head, polished to a shine. "That's a second-story man out of Baltimore, named Chrome Lasker. Why don't we ask him what's going on?"

The Hardys pushed through the crowd, closing in on Lasker. The bald man didn't notice them. He was busy speaking to a guy in a white suit. In profile, the second man had a thick mustache and what looked like tiny, ratlike eyes.

"Lasker," Frank said, clamping a hand on the bald man's shoulder. Without missing a beat, the mustached man clipped Frank with a massive hand, knocking him down. The two men took off running.

"They're heading for the exit," Joe said as he helped Frank to his feet. Frank looked down the corridor where the two men had gone. It ended in double doors.

"That's not an exit," Frank said. "It leads to a service area. We've got them cornered. Come on."

They pushed through the double doors into darkness. As the doors slammed shut behind them, each of the Hardys felt something thin and cool wrap around his throat. Frank and Joe felt hot breath raise the hairs on the backs of their necks. The men behind them were taller than they were, and, if they could go by the grip the men had, they were a lot bigger too.

Wires held in strong hands tightened and began to bite into the Hardys' throats, slowly squeezing the life out of them.

Chapter

4

JOE HARDY RAISED a foot and brought it down as hard as he could on the toes of the man strangling him. The man howled and loosened his grip on the wire. Joe rammed an elbow into the man's stomach.

Pain shot through Joe's arm, as if he'd just smashed into a rock. With a grunt and a laugh, the man rapped Joe on the side of the head, knocking the younger Hardy off his feet. The wire caught him around the neck again and tightened.

Joe dangled there, trying to brace his feet again, feeling his weight drag him into the strangling wire. His pulse pounded in his ears, and his lungs burned for air. Nearby, he watched Frank struggle, with no more success than he was having.

Something—a foot, Joe figured—smacked into the back of his knees, knocking his legs out from under him. He knew the man holding the wire wasn't about to let him get his balance again.

There was a click, and instantly light streamed through the darkness and widened. A woman's shadow fell across them, but Joe, almost unconscious, could see nothing. He heard two dull thuds, and air rushed into his lungs as he fell to the floor and the wire slid from his neck.

"Frank!" Joe called as he wobbled to his feet. "You all right?"

Next to him, Frank rolled over and sat up, coughing and rubbing his neck. "I'm okay. What happened?"

Joe looked at his and his brother's attackers lying at their feet. They weren't the men the Hardys had been following, but rather tan, muscular giants. One had a tattoo of an anchor on his forearm. Both were unconscious now, sprawled on the floor.

"Sailors of some sort, I'd guess." Joe's voice croaked out of a throat that still stung from the bite of the wire. "When the doors opened, there was this shadow, and—"

"Charity!" they said at the same time.

"I'm starting to get real tired of her." Frank fumed.

But Joe wasn't listening. He was out the door and back in the main terminal, looking for any sign of Charity. Other planes had unloaded passengers, and the terminal was filled. If Charity was there, Joe realized, she would be well hidden by the crowd.

"Kid!" a voice nearby called out, followed by murmured protests from the passersby on Joe's left. He turned to see what the commotion was about.

A heavyset man with a round face was pushing against the flow of the crowd, jostling people in his hurry to get to Joe. He smiled and waved, and Joe thought about turning tail and running. But it was too late. The cheery man clasped Joe's hand and shook it fiercely. Joe stared at the man, puzzled.

"Kid!" the man cried. "Don't you recognize me? It's Jolly!"

"Jolly?" Joe replied.

The man named Jolly nudged him in the ribs and lowered his voice. "Sure. You remember. That job we pulled on the French Riviera?"

"Oh," Joe answered, smiling nervously. "The French Riviera job. How've you been?"

Jolly winked at him. "I don't blame you for not recognizing me. We only met once, and that was a good ten years ago. But I never forget a face, kid." He ran a finger along Joe's cheek and nodded admiringly. "Great lift job. I can only just make out the scars.

"As for how I've been, well, it's been slow. I was thinking of getting a real job when this came up." For a moment Jolly's face fell into a frown, but then the smile returned. "A score like this should put us both on easy street for the rest of our lives. You want to ride with me to the meet?"

Joe glanced over his shoulder. Frank stood against a wall, watching them with the same puzzled expression that Joe felt he must have. Joe shrugged slightly and caught Frank's eye. Nodding, Frank faded back.

"Sure," Joe said.

Jolly led him out of the airport to the taxi stand, talking about old times and old scores. Joe decided to let Jolly do the talking, since Joe didn't have the slightest idea what he was talking about.

He settled back in the cab, listening to Jolly and wondering where they were going.

The cab pulled up in front of a warehouse along the docks on San Diego's Embarcadero. "Sure this is where you want to go?" the driver asked. "This place has been shut down for years."

"Sure I'm sure," Jolly said, handing the

driver a twenty-dollar bill. "Keep the change, pal."

As the taxi drove off, Joe looked around. The street was all warehouses, but to the northwest Joe could see the tall buildings of downtown San Diego. Behind the warehouses was the shining blue of San Diego Bay; he could smell the ocean in the air.

"This way," Jolly said, gesturing toward a warehouse with a steel door painted red. "Didn't they give you instructions?"

"Let's just say I had to leave the dump where I was staying in a hurry," Joe lied. "Everything got left behind, including my luggage and the instructions."

"Well, that's one of the hazards," Jolly said. He pulled open the warehouse door.

Joe was expecting darkness inside, but instead the warehouse was filled with a soft blue light. "Come in," said a deep voice. They went in, letting the door close softly behind them.

A tall man stood just inside. He wore an expensive gray silk suit, white-on-white shirt, and a deadly gleam in his eye. A razor-thin scar, dead white, traced a line on his tanned face from the bottom of his left ear to the corner of his mouth. As he turned to face the newcomers, the outline of a large gun in a shoulder holster showed in the fabric of his suit coat.

"Names?" he asked with a faint Hispanic accent.

"I'm Jolly," Jolly said. He clapped a hand on Joe's shoulder. "This is my main man, the Kid. We're expected."

The scarred man nodded but didn't smile. "You're the last. Go in."

Joe and Jolly stepped past him, and the man followed them into the warehouse. A dozen or more men stood there, or sat on crates. No one spoke. Their eyes were riveted on a five-foot projection television screen that hung from the ceiling. The screen, empty of any picture but still on, was the source of the blue light.

The scarred man stepped in front of the screen and clapped his hands twice. All eyes were on him. "Greetings," he said. "I am Chavo. Your host, my employer, will join us shortly.

"You, gentlemen—and lady—are the world's finest thieves. Perhaps the best that ever were. You all know why we are gathered here. If we are successful, we will all be rich beyond our wildest dreams. This means that we must work together, without fear of betrayal. Is there anyone here who feels he can't do that?"

A short man with red hair piped up. "I don't trust anyone I've never met. The name's Brady."

"Everest," the man next to him said.

The next man stood up, the blue light bouncing off his shiny skull, and Joe swallowed hard. It was Chrome Lasker. But Lasker stared straight at Joe and identified himself. There was nothing in his face. Their two-second encounter at the airport hadn't been enough for him to recognize Joe.

" 'Cat' Willeford," said the man sitting on the crate with him, and Joe recognized Willeford as the mustached man who'd been talking to Lasker at the airport.

It went on and on, until everyone had identified himself.

Then Jolly stepped forward, bowing to the crowd as if they were an audience. "The name's Jolly," he said, "specialist in all things crystal and silver. And this"—he pointed at Joe—"is the Kid."

Everyone was growing bored by then, but at the mention of the Kid's name, all heads popped up, eyeing him.

"You got to a score just before I did," Everest growled.

"Sorry about that," Joe said, clenching his fists. He could feel a fight coming on.

"Forget it," Everest replied, and his scowl turned to a smile. "Just don't cut me out of this one, or . . ." He ran a fingernail across his throat, leaving a bright red streak. Joe nodded.

"Don't let him throw you, Kid," Brady said admiringly. "You're a legend. We study your capers.

"Now," Chavo continued, "if there's nothing else . . ."

"Don't forget me," said a melodic voice, and Joe's blood ran cold. From the shadows stepped Charity, dressed now in a blouse and skirt. Calmly she strolled across the room, moving toward Joe.

He stood still, not knowing what to do as she said, "Someone here is hiding something."

The rest of the thieves in the room began to move, some nervous, some scowling. Several slipped things out of pockets—knives, blackjacks, brass knuckles—the weapons of their trade. Joe knew that when Charity fingered him, the others would descend on him and tear him to pieces. She kept walking, moving steadily toward him.

"I know," she said as she put her arms around Joe's neck, "who you really are."

Chapter

5

JOE'S STOMACH KNOTTED as if a fist had been driven into it, but to Joe's surprise, Charity leaned over and kissed his cheek. Putting an arm around his waist, she swung back to face the others. A shiver ran through him, and he tried to breathe, but he couldn't. He could feel the hot breath of death on his face.

"The Kid and I pulled a caper together once. We got very close. I even learned his *real* name." She flashed him a catlike smile.

"You can't," Joe muttered, but he knew she wouldn't listen. He flexed his fingers, determined to take as many of them with him as possible.

"The Kid's real name is Crawford Laird Pulansky."

For a moment Joe couldn't understand what he had heard. She had lied for him! Why? Relief and shock washed over him, and his legs grew rubbery, but he locked his knees and forced himself to stand.

"Crawford." One of the thieves let out a guffaw. Then everyone in the room was roaring with laughter, until Chavo clapped his hands again. "If we are done with the entertainment portion of our program . . ."

Joe leaned over to Charity and whispered, "Is that the Kid's real name?"

"How should I know?" Charity whispered back. "I never met the guy."

Chavo hit a switch. A tiny dot of light formed in the center of the video screen and spread out until it formed a picture. It was a head and shoulders, but Joe couldn't tell if it was a man or a woman. The face on the screen was covered by a brown hood. Joe guessed that eyeholes had been cut into it, because the brown hood had dark glasses over the eyes. The voice was scrambled electronically, so it came out sounding like a robot's voice.

"Welcome," it said. "Welcome to the perfect crime. You may call me the Director."

The crooks began to murmur, but Chavo shouted, "Silence!" and they turned their attention back to the screen.

"For reasons of security, I can't tell you

where we are going to strike, or when. The operation will be divided into sections. Chavo will tell you who is needed, and for what.

"I want to thank everyone for being here. I can guarantee that if you follow instructions, this venture will be satisfactorily profitable for everyone.

"Now, go have a good day, see San Diego if you wish, stay out of trouble, and be back here at nine this evening. That is all."

The light blinked out, and the screen went dead.

Joe stood there for a moment, staring at the screen in bewilderment. What *have* I stumbled into? he wondered. He decided that, for the moment, it wasn't important. The first thing he had to do was bring in Charity. She was right beside him, and he could walk out with her now and she wouldn't be able to say a word. If this band of cutthroats ever got the idea that she had lied to them, she'd be dead. He had a hold on her.

But when he turned to grab Charity, she was gone.

He joined the others as they filed out into the street and looked all around. Again, no sign of Charity.

But he did notice something he'd missed before. On top of the warehouse was a satellite television dish.

"So, want to hang out with me today?" he heard Jolly say.

"Thanks," Joe replied. "But I've got a lot of things to do. Buy some new clothes, rent a room—"

"Yeah," Jolly agreed. "I understand. That would take up a lot of time. Well, I'll see you again tonight." He walked off.

Joe hoped Frank had managed to follow them. He wished he could talk to Frank now, but the others were still too close. If Frank contacted him now, it could be fatal for both of them.

He walked down the street, heading for the buildings in the distance. No sign of Frank on the empty streets. Here and there he passed other people, but they paid no attention to him.

Only one man nodded at Joe as he passed, a man in slacks and shirtsleeves, with his coat draped over his arm. Looking at the guy, Joe realized for the first time how hot he was himself. The weather had been cooling off in Bayport, but in San Diego it was just like summer.

Joe continued looking for any sign of Frank but saw none. He did see the man with the coat over his arm again. There was something strangely familiar about the guy.

No one I've met, Joe decided. The guy was blond haired and blue eyed, just over six feet tall, broad and muscular. From a distance he looked like a teenager, but as he came closer, Joe saw the man's looks could be the result of cosmetic surgery. Joe knew he was much older than his unlined face would indicate.

"Excuse me. Do you have the time?" the man asked, stopping next to Joe.

Joe raised his arm to look at his watch, and started to say, "A little after—" when he felt a heavy nudge in his ribs.

"That's a Smith and Wesson persuader in your side," the man said in a low, deadly calm voice. Out of the corner of his eye Joe caught the dark polished glint of gunmetal. "Walk."

"I don't have much money on me," Joe began, but another nudge shut him up.

"This isn't about money," the man said. "Make a move and I'll blow you away. Just do what I tell you." The man shoved Joe toward a car parked at the curb.

"I'll make any move I want," Joe threatened. "You wouldn't dare shoot me in front of other people."

The man sneered. "I'm a little crazy, see? Someone takes my name, I don't care *what* I have to do to deal with it."

Joe's heart jumped to his throat. It was the real Kid!

"You drive," the Kid said as they got into the car. "It's a nice day for a trip to the zoo."

Joe studied the Kid as they drove off. The Kid was good-looking, but Joe couldn't understand how anyone would mistake the two of them.

Frantically, Frank Hardy flagged down a cab after his brother had been forced into a waiting car. Frank had been tailing Joe since the airport, but he hadn't been able to get close enough to figure out what was going on.

"Follow that car," he told the driver as he got into the cab. He bit down lightly on his tongue when he heard himself say it. He pointed out the Chevy.

When the driver heard Frank's order, he cried, "Far out, man! I've been waiting to have someone say that all my life." The cabbie had long, stringy hair and a set of beads around his neck. Frank thought he looked like something out of the 1960s.

The San Diego Zoo was one of the largest in the world, set in the middle of the twelve hundred acres of Balboa Park, just north of downtown San Diego. The zoo contained more than thirty-two hundred animals, separated by moats and fences from the thousands of people who visited the park daily. Much of the environment looked like a tropical jungle.

Joe Hardy wasn't interested in the animals.

The Kid had herded him through the main entrance, toward the aerial tram ride that ran above the park from this side to the other, a third of a mile away. The trolley cars held only two people each. The cars were so light that they swayed on the thin cable they hung from.

"Get on," the Kid muttered in Joe's ear as he handed their tickets to the young woman who loaded the trolleys. She opened the car door and closed it after them. Then, with a jerk, the cable pulled their car up into the air and out over the zoo.

"Nice view, isn't it?" The Kid brought the gun out into the open, his finger still wrapped around the trigger. The nose was pointed at Joe.

"Are we up here for my health?" Joe asked.

"Yeah," the Kid replied. "Time to improve your physical fitness. You're going to practice high dives."

Joe looked down, his stomach pulling tight. They were at least seventy-five feet up, swaying between the concrete path below and the animal pens on either side of them.

"You're crazy," Joe said.

"Never say that to the man with the gun," said the Kid. "The way I figure it, you're big, but not too big for me to toss into a bear or tiger cage as we go over. The fall will probably

41

kill you, but if it doesn't, the animals will get to you before help can."

Joe gripped the safety bar and held on tight. "What if I just promise never to use your name again?"

The Kid shook his head. "Too late."

The butt of the gun suddenly smashed into Joe's jaw. Hold on, he told himself as a gray cloud fogged into his mind. Hold on!

Strong hands gripped Joe diagonally around his waist and shoulders. He tried to move his arms to fight, but they wouldn't work. The gray cloud moved in, swallowing all thought.

Standing up in the trolley, the Kid lifted Joe over his head as if he were a doll, ready to heave the younger Hardy into the bear pits far below.

Chapter

6

FRANK HARDY GOT OUT of the cab and followed his brother and the blond guy. He'd been trying to catch Joe's eye, but the other man always got between them.

The stranger looked more like Joe's brother than Frank did, Frank realized suddenly with a shock. They obviously weren't identical, but in the right light, facing someone who knew neither of them very well, they could easily be mistaken for each other.

The two of them got into a tram car and lifted off, heading for the other end of the park. Frank jogged along the walkway beneath the trolley line, keeping his eyes on the car overhead.

"Joe!" he called out, but the trolley was too far up. There was no way Joe could hear him.

The car began to sway too violently to be caused by the wind. Something was happening up there, but Frank couldn't tell what. He sprinted ahead of it, turning and looking up to get a glimpse of the inside of the car. The angle was all wrong. He couldn't see.

Then a dark mass tipped over the lip of the car. It struck the pavement with a dull thud and rolled over once, landing in a position impossible for a living man.

All the color drained from Frank's face. He recognized the body.

It was Joe.

Frank sank to his knees next to his brother. He didn't care about anything, not Charity, the Star of Ishtar, Chief Collig, or the people gathering around them. All that mattered was that his brother was dead.

As tears filled his eyes, he froze, startled. There were little marks next to Joe's ears, tiny, almost invisible scratches he assumed were caused by the fall. He looked at them more closely, and his heart raced.

The marks were old—scars. Joe never had any scars around his ears.

It was the other man, he realized with a thrill. It *wasn't* Joe!

His eyes darted up at the trolley car that was

vanishing into the distance. Frank sprinted past the people coming to stare at the body, shaking off hands that reached out to stop him.

"You can't go," someone shouted. "What happened?"

"He fell," Frank yelled back over his shoulder. He didn't want to talk. He needed the air for running. "Call the police."

He reached the trolley car as it was coming to a stop at the far end of the line. Joe, still woozy, staggered out of the car, and Frank, still running, threw his arms around Joe and hugged him.

"You sound a little winded," Joe said as Frank tried to keep his legs from buckling under him.

Puffing, Frank said, "I've just run three hundred-yard dashes back-to-back, and I think I set records. What happened? Who *was* that guy?"

"That was the Kid—the crook that guy Jolly took me for. He was about to throw me off the car, but I managed to get a grip on the roof. I held on. He lurched forward, but I stayed where I was, and he pitched off the car. I barely made it back into the seat before I blacked out."

"We don't have to worry about the Kid anymore," Frank said. "But we'd better get out of here before the police arrive."

"Good idea," Joe said. Hiding behind bushes, they scaled the tall back wall and dropped down to the street behind the zoo. As police cars roared past, sirens blaring, they walked calmly down the sidewalk, heading back downtown.

Relaxing, Frank asked, "So how did you get mixed up with the Kid?"

"A gang I ran into at the warehouse thinks I'm him," Joe said. "He didn't like that." He looked over his shoulder, checking for the police before continuing. There was no sign of them.

"So what did you learn? What's going on?"

"It's all pretty confusing," Joe replied. "Apparently all those thieves we saw at the airport have gotten together for a big heist. It's being planned by someone calling himself the Director, but I don't know who he—or she—is. He wears a mask and talks to us on television." Joe's face brightened. "Hey! You're good with computers and electronics. Is there any way we could trace where the TV signal's coming from?"

Frank shook his head. "Only if it's a direct cable feed. If he's using a satellite dish, he's bouncing the signal off a satellite. It could be coming from anywhere."

"Then the only way to crack this scheme is for me to keep pretending to be the Kid."

"No," Frank said. "It's too dangerous. You'd be completely on your own."

"You'll be nearby," Joe protested. "Besides, Charity's in with them."

When he heard that name, Frank gave his brother a look. He let out a weary sigh, and, after thinking a long time, said, "All right. But be careful." He thought a moment more. "Let's get a hotel room and some food. Then later we should go to the warehouse and check it out before the gang gets back."

"Outside of this TV projection screen and the cable leading to the dish on the roof, it's an ordinary warehouse," Frank said. He and Joe had been there for several hours, scouring the place from top to bottom. It was clean. "We'd better get out of here."

Joe stiffened just then, listening. A dozen pairs of footsteps were headed their way outside. "Too late," he said. "They're here. Better hide."

Frank glanced around. The only place to hide in the warehouse was behind the crates, and Joe had told him that the gang would be sitting on them. He needed a hiding place they wouldn't find, somewhere they wouldn't go.

Moments later the gang entered the room, with Chavo bringing up the rear. Chuckling, Jolly walked up to Joe as the others seated themselves around the projection TV. "I take it we're about to embark on our little project."

Charity pressed herself between them and slipped her arm into Joe's arm. "Mind if I borrow him?" she asked Jolly, batting her eyes sweetly at him. Then, before the heavy man could answer, she pulled Joe away. They sat down together in front of the screen, his arm firmly locked in hers.

"Mind yourself and don't say a thing," she whispered in his ear. "There's a big surprise coming." Joe clenched his jaw angrily but kept quiet.

Chavo switched the screen back on, and once again the covered face of the Director appeared on it. "We are about to begin," the electronic voice droned.

"By tomorrow morning you will all be millionaires. Half of you will receive instructions from Chavo for later tonight. The other operatives, whose names I am about to read, will assemble at the boat moored behind this warehouse. On the boat, you will get your orders for an invasion of the Point Loma Naval Station."

Several of the criminals stood up, yelling in disbelief. Chavo stepped in front of the screen and stared at them with those cruel, piercing eyes. His hand slipped into his coat pocket and pressed the shape of a pistol against the fabric so everyone could see. The criminals quieted down.

"Now," the Director continued, "the assault group will be co-commanded by Charity and Willeford. It has been carefully planned, and if all the instructions are followed to the letter, no one will be hurt." He rattled off a list of names, and, after a long pause that sent a shiver down Joe's spine, ended the list with "the Kid."

"Go now," he said. "And good luck."

Charity pulled Joe out of the warehouse toward the mooring, with the rest of their crew following them. Joe still said nothing, but now his silence sprang from anger.

"Cheer up," she said as if she had read his mind. "It'll be fun."

They climbed onto the boat, a small cabin cruiser.

Behind the screen, Frank listened and waited for all the footsteps to die away. He realized he'd been sweating. All through the meeting, he had been pressed up against the screen, hoping not to be noticed. But what he had heard alarmed him. He had to warn the police and the navy of what was about to happen, and he hoped Joe would be able to protect himself. Cautiously Frank stepped to the front of the screen.

It came on with a loud click, and he found

himself face-to-face with the TV image of the Director. A gun barrel nuzzled against the back of Frank's neck.

"You're caught, spy," the Director said.

"Hands up," Chavo said. Frank put them up.

"I thought you were on tape," Frank told the man. "You sure fooled everyone."

"They think what I want them to think," said the Director. "What's your connection with the other spy?"

"I don't know what you're talking about," Frank said.

"The one who claims to be the Kid," the Director replied. "The real Kid was found today in the San Diego Zoo. I'm afraid he's in no condition to help our little operation. The impostor, I'm afraid, will be in for a rude surprise—after he has outlived his usefulness."

"Why, you—" Frank began, but before he could move, Chavo punched him in the small of the back, doubling him over. The scarred man waved the barrel of a silenced .45 in front of Frank's nose.

"Take him out back," the Director told Chavo, "and shoot him."

The boat pulled away from its mooring and sped out into the dark night. Moodily Joe leaned against the back rail of the boat, staring back at the well-lit dock they had just left. I've got to figure a way out of this, he thought. But he could think of nothing except leaping overboard, and then he'd never be able to stop the caper that was going down.

Joe's jaw dropped and a tiny cry burst from him. From out of nowhere, Charity appeared.

Joe shouted, "We've got to go back. Right now. Look at the dock!" He turned his eyes back to the land, but he knew he would be too late already.

Chavo had marched Frank to the end of the pier, overlooking the water. "Turn around," he ordered. Frank turned, his heels over the edge of the pier.

With a chuckle, Chavo pressed the silenced gun against Frank's chest. A noise that sounded like a loud sneeze erupted twice from the gun.

Frank toppled backward, hit the water, and slowly sank beneath the waves.

Chapter

7

JOE WOULD HAVE SCREAMED, but Charity had
clamped her hand over his mouth. He felt like
leaping off the boat and swimming to his brother's side, but Charity whispered to him, "It's
too late for Frank. There's nothing you can do
to help him."

He tore himself free, wanting to strike out at
something, anything, to avenge his brother. Joe
clenched his fists, calculating how many men
were on board and what chance he'd have
against them if he took them all on.

None, he realized. He might take down one
or two, but the rest would get him, and they'd
have no qualms about killing him as Frank had
been killed. Joe had to stay in the game if he

wanted to nail the ones really responsible for Frank's death.

Beside him, Charity was shaking, a look of horror on her face. Like Joe, she was still staring back at the one brightly lit dock, at the last place they had seen Frank.

"I'm so sorry," she said. "It wasn't supposed to go like this."

"What did you have in mind?" Joe snarled, not really interested.

"We can't talk here," she said. "Things aren't what they seem." Almost as an afterthought she added, "You'll have to trust me."

On a boat full of killers and thieves, Joe knew he had no other choice.

Frank Hardy struggled woozily, spitting water from his mouth. He had a dull ache in his chest, and he was soaked to the skin. Where was he? His hands were clinging to something round and wooden, so damp that the wood was flaking off in wads of soggy pulp. He opened his eyes.

He remembered the pier, and the last words Chavo had spoken as they walked to the end of it. "This will hurt, but go along with it. Act like you've been shot. Stay under the pier until I can come for you. You'll have to trust me."

Now Frank was under the pier, hidden by it, clinging to one of the poles holding it up, water up to his ribs. Above, he heard slow, deliberate footsteps, then a cold Hispanic voice. "Frank Hardy?"

It was Chavo.

Frank thought about hiding there, waiting until Chavo had gone. What did he know about the man? Nothing. Why should he trust him? There was no reason.

Except Chavo had saved his life. Why? What was Chavo's game?

Frank climbed up the rough planks that had been nailed onto the pole as a makeshift ladder. As he reached the top of the pier, Chavo reached down and offered him a hand.

"Are you all right?" Chavo asked as Frank knelt on one knee and caught his breath.

"I've been better," Frank said. "You didn't need to use the rubber bullets. If you weren't going to shoot me, you could've aimed a little to my left."

Chavo laughed. "Yes, but it wouldn't have been as convincing. The Director had to be convinced."

"Do you have some special reason for double-crossing your boss?"

Chavo produced a badge. "Don't you want to thank me for saving your life?"

"Thanks," Frank said as he studied the badge. "Federales. Mexican National Police.

Does our government know you're working out of San Diego?"

"No. You understand my position. I infiltrated the Director's gang months ago. I must go where I am sent, and no one knows who I really am."

"Pretty good infiltration job," Frank said. "You made it all the way to number-two man."

"*Sí*. I recruited the others on his orders. But he does not trust me. Like the others, I receive my orders in pieces. No one but the Director knows everything he is planning."

Frank stared at the Mexican lawman. "How do you know who I am? You called me by name."

"The other one was identified as Joseph Hardy," Chavo replied. "I don't think you could be your illustrious father, so who else would you be but Frank?"

"You know Dad?"

"I know of him," Chavo said. He led Frank toward the land. "Come. The others have been sent to Tijuana, in Mexico, to wait for more instructions. We must hurry."

"I'm soaking wet!" Frank protested.

Chavo looked grim. "You'll find a change of clothes in my car. We must warn the Naval Station of the coming attack. There is no time to waste."

Frank studied the face of the scarred man,

but it told him nothing. Was Chavo an undercover agent, trained to keep himself a closed book? Or simply a clever crook looking to double-cross his boss?

Frank had no way to tell, but he agreed with Chavo on one thing: the navy had to be warned. With doubts he followed Chavo up the pier to the waiting car.

Willeford stepped onto the deck as the boat cruised in toward the rocks under Point Loma Naval Station. The entire area was fenced in, and from high towers, spotlights swept across the water. The cabin cruiser came to a halt just outside the range of the lights, and Willeford cut the motor. The boat drifted silently on the waves.

"How are we supposed to crack that place?" someone asked.

Instead of answering, Willeford took a sealed envelope from his pocket and ran a thumbnail through the seal. Pulling a paper out, he whispered, "Everyone quiet. Want the whole navy to hear us?" The criminals sat in silence as Willeford carefully read the instructions.

"There are two inflatable rubber rafts being dragged behind the boat. They're fitted with outboard motors, and are small and quick enough to dodge the spotlights." He held up a small photograph and passed it around. "This is where you go ashore."

The photo reached Joe, who saw that it showed the rocks under the base, with one area marked by an arrow drawn with a felt-tip pen.

"Climb up those rocks. You'll find specially drilled hand- and footholds. At the top, you'll meet a sailor." Willeford rubbed his fingers against his palm and grinned savagely, and Joe got the idea. Someone had been paid off to get them into the base.

"What happens then? What are we doing?" one of the guys asked.

"You'll learn more as you need to know it," Willeford answered, staring the guy down. "Everyone ready?"

There was some murmuring, but it wasn't long before everyone was set to go. If this operation worked out the way the Director planned, it would be a cinch, and even Joe knew it.

The rubber rafts cut the water like speed-boats, leaving nothing but waves for the spotlights to light up. Their motors were specially muffled to keep the sound to a minimum, and it wasn't long before they were at the rocks. The holds were exactly where the Director had said they'd be, and one by one the gang climbed the rocks to the base.

A guard stood there, glaring down at them, aiming his rifle. "Who goes there?" he asked menacingly.

The criminals froze, faced with the gun muzzle.

Willeford piped up, "Blackjack."

A nervous smile crossed the guard's lips, and he lowered his rifle and stepped aside. "Pass." The guard had his shirtsleeves rolled up, and Joe recognized the anchor tattoo on his forearm. He was one of the two men who'd tried to strangle him and Frank at the airport.

The guard stepped back to the fence and pulled out a section.

In a line, like commandos, the raiders scrambled onto the sleeping base. They clung to the shadows as the occasional jeep went by, but they met no one.

"The fleet's out on maneuvers," the guard explained as they approached a gray metal hut with No Admittance stenciled on the door in huge letters. "The base is working with a skeleton crew." He jangled keys, then put one in the lock. The door swung open.

Swiftly they swarmed inside and shut the door behind them and flipped the light switch to on. "What you're looking for is over there," the guard said. Following the beam from the guard's flashlight, Joe saw racks and racks of metal drums.

"Some of this is poison gas," Joe said, dread creeping into his voice. "You breathe this long enough and you're dead."

"We need some of that poison," Willeford replied, looking at his orders. "This stuff has been stored here because no one could figure out what else to do with it. Everyone grab a canister and let's move out."

The criminals scrambled through the hut, lifting the drums off the racks. Joe was worried. Nerve gas was something he didn't want to fool with. In the darkness, he looked for another way out. There was none but the door, where the guard now stood.

"Where's Charity?" Joe asked, realizing she wasn't with them.

"Forget her," Willeford ordered, but he scowled as he spoke. "Do your job."

Joe spotted a different canister, one marked Knockout Gas. Quickly he plucked it off the rack, covering the name with his arm, and carried it on his shoulder.

"Come on!" Willeford barked, checking his watch. "We're running behind schedule. Move it." As one, they started for the door.

It swung open suddenly, and there stood a sailor. He was young and bewildered by the activity. "What's going on here?" he asked.

The guard grabbed him and punched him once in the stomach, doubling him over. As the guard twisted the sailor's arm behind his back and dragged him into the hut, Willeford came forward and put a gun to the back of the sailor's head.

"Too bad you stumbled into this," Willeford said, and cocked back the trigger.

"You can't!" Joe shouted, before he realized what he was saying.

All eyes were on him, and Willeford's eyes turned to dark, murderous slits in his face. "Going soft, Kid?" He pulled another gun from his belt and tossed it to Joe. "I think you'd better take care of him."

Joe hesitated, staring at the pleading eyes of the sailor.

Angrily Willeford aimed his gun at Joe. "I don't think you understand me, Kid. You don't have a choice. We can't afford to have this sailor boy running around to tell about our business. Kill him."

His eyes were icy cold. "Or *I* kill *you*."

Chapter

8

"OF COURSE he has to die," Joe growled angrily.

Willeford hesitantly lowered his gun.

"But a shot might bring the whole base down on us. How about we run a little test on him?" Joe raised the canister he held, keeping the label against his chest. He knew the gas wouldn't cause severe injury to the sailor. "How about we give him a sniff of this?"

"Please, no!" the sailor pleaded. "I won't say anything. I swear."

"I like your style, Kid," Willeford said. "Everybody out."

Joe handed the gun back to Willeford as he passed and lifted his canister so the nozzle on it was aimed at the sailor. Turning his head away, Joe opened the valve, and a thin spray of white gas rushed into the sailor's face.

"Close that thing," Willeford said from outside, fear in his voice. His eyes were on the sailor, who gasped and clawed at his throat, trying to get words out. They stuck in his throat.

The sailor toppled forward, to land facedown on the floor. Willeford walked back in and nudged the body with his toe: the young seaman didn't move.

"Good work, Kid," Willeford said, going back out. "I misjudged you."

Cautiously the guard led the criminals from the hut. Before he left, Joe looked back at the sailor, who still hadn't stirred. In the dark, Joe could just see the sailor's chest steadily rise and fall. The man was breathing, and Joe felt a wave of relief.

Now all he had to do was keep himself alive and figure out what had happened to Charity.

"The admiral's not available," the military policeman at the front gate of the naval base said.

Chavo held up his badge, and the MP grinned. "This isn't Mexico, pal. Come back tomorrow."

"You don't understand," Frank said. "Your base is being robbed."

That raised the MP's eyebrows. He rested his hand on the automatic in his holster. "I think you two had better wait here. The officer in charge will want to talk to you."

The MP went into the little booth at the gate and spoke briefly on the phone, keeping his eyes on Frank and Chavo. Moments later a jeep rolled up to the gate, and two MPs leapt out, followed by a white-haired man in a uniform marked by the silver-eagle insignia of a navy captain. The MPs stood at ease as the captain approached the gate.

"Let them in," the captain said, and the MP on guard swung the gate open. Chavo and Frank tensely walked in. "I'm Captain Hammond. You were saying something about a burglary on base?"

"There's a gang of men stealing something here," Frank said, but Chavo stepped between him and Hammond and held up his credentials again.

Captain Hammond shook him off. "You understand that I'll have to call your superiors and learn if you're who you say you are. There are procedures to follow."

"There's no time," Frank insisted. "The heist is happening right now."

"I cannot permit you to check with my superiors," Chavo admitted. "I am on special undercover assignment. It is essential that my cover not be blown. This matter must remain strictly between us.''

''That's not possible,'' Captain Hammond replied. ''Frankly, I don't believe either one of you. There's nothing on this base worth stealing. We have no real money, and all the weapons are stored over on North Island.'' His eyes widened slightly. ''Unless—''

''Sir?'' an MP said, noting the look of concern on the captain's face.

''Into the jeep,'' Captain Hammond suddenly ordered. He pointed at Chavo and Frank. ''You too.'' They clambered in.

''Where to, sir?'' the MP who was driving asked, shifting the jeep into low gear.

''The gas depository,'' the captain said gravely. ''If someone got his hands on that . . .''

''Nerve gas?'' Frank said. ''I thought the government didn't make that anymore.''

''This is old, but just as dangerous as it was when it was created,'' Hammond replied. ''We store it here because there's no safe way to get rid of it.'' He turned to look at Frank. ''Who are you, anyway? You don't look Mexican.''

''I'm American, sir,'' Frank replied. ''I ran into this business from a different direction than Chavo.''

''And you don't want to identify yourself either,'' Captain Hammond interrupted.

"Plenty of time for that later, I suppose. You two aren't going anywhere."

The jeep approached the hut where the nerve gas was stored, and the captain's face turned to stone. The door to the hut was wide open, and just inside, lit up by the jeep's headlights, a sailor lay flat on the floor.

Frank leapt from the jeep and ran into the hut. He crouched and laid a hand on the sailor's neck. "I'm getting a pulse." Gently he patted the sailor's cheek. As Captain Hammond, Chavo, and the two MPs entered and stood above them, the sailor's eyes fluttered open.

"What happened here, man?" Captain Hammond demanded.

The sailor told the story as if he couldn't believe he was alive.

"They couldn't have gotten far," Captain Hammond said. To one MP he said, "I want the entire base on alert. Do a full perimeter check. Well, what are you standing there for? Go!"

He scowled as he looked at Chavo and Frank, and as he faced the other MP, he waved his thumb at them.

"Place these two under arrest."

*   *   *

Joe had barely climbed back in the rubber raft, setting his cargo on his lap, when an alarm sounded on the base.

"We've been discovered," Willeford shouted. "Move it." The man handling the outboard motor pulled on the crank and brought it to life. The raft zipped across the bay, heading back to the cabin cruiser. Nearby, Joe could see the other raft, keeping pace with them.

Then a spotlight caught the other raft, and Joe looked over his shoulder at the shore. All along the cliff, men were lining up, and in the moonlight Joe caught the glint of rifles in their hands.

"Stop those craft immediately!" commanded a booming voice over a loudspeaker. "Do not move. This will be your only warning!"

"Keep going," Willeford shouted.

Joe ducked down as a hail of bullets rained down around them in the water. In the other raft, still caught in the spotlight, one man clutched at his shoulder, screamed, and tumbled into the black water. Suddenly there was a blast like a gigantic balloon popping.

A shot had punctured the other raft. One whole side had blown open, and the raft began to sink. The desperate criminals threw their canisters overboard and abandoned ship. They swam off the sinking raft and moved toward Joe's raft.

"We don't need them," Willeford said, and they took off, leaving the stranded criminals behind. Joe realized the raft had moved out of firing range.

Moments later the raft reached the cabin cruiser, and Willeford climbed aboard while everyone else stayed in the raft. One by one, the others climbed the rope ladder leading to the boat, leaving only Joe in the raft. He handed the canisters up to them, and they handed them man to man like firefighters handing off buckets of water, until all the canisters were on board.

"Stay there," Willeford called down to Joe, as he pulled the ladder up.

"What's going on?" Joe asked, and Willeford popped his head over the edge of the cabin cruiser and beamed a friendly smile down at him. Joe shivered.

Willeford held out a package. "This is the last of the Director's orders for this operation. Catch." He dropped the package, and Joe caught it.

It was small, about the size of a roll of film, and tightly wrapped in brown paper. "Take it back to the warehouse and give it to Chavo," Willeford continued. "You'll get your next order there. We're heading out."

Joe acknowledged the order with a brief nod, then turned the raft away from the boat and sped off into the night toward the dock. He was glad he'd finally gotten away from the others. Now he'd have a chance to face Chavo and make him pay for what he had done to Frank.

The cabin cruiser sped out of the bay and into the Pacific Ocean. Back at the base, the shooting had stopped. The night was quiet now, as if nothing had happened.

The outboard motor hummed a deep staccato tune, uneven enough to keep Joe from being lulled to sleep. As he listened, he began to notice a second, higher-pitched whine of another motor.

Someone was following him.

"Joe!" a woman's voice cried. He looked over to see Charity pulling alongside, piloting a speedboat. Between the noise of the two engines, nothing else could be heard. Charity signaled for Joe to shut off his motor. He did.

"You have to get off the raft!" she yelled.

"What?"

She gritted her teeth and waved at him to jump. "They know who you are. You have to get off that raft—"

"They're gone, Captain," the MP told Hammond, and Hammond frowned. He stood on the cliff, looking down at the frantic scene below. Half a dozen men were splashing in the water below, waiting for help.

"Call the Coast Guard and have them search for the boat," Hammond said. "Fish those men out and have them arrested."

A sailor with a pair of binoculars waved them at Hammond. "There's something else out there, sir. Some kind of a raft."

Captain Hammond reached for the binoculars, but Frank, who had been brought there with Chavo so Hammond could keep his eye on them, stepped forward and grabbed them. Hammond started to give another order, but Frank explained, "My brother's out there somewhere. I have to know what happened to him."

He scanned the sea. Joe wasn't among the men in the water, and Frank turned his gaze on the raft. He grinned with excitement.

Joe was standing up in the raft.

"It's Joe," he said happily, and handed the binoculars to Hammond.

A few minutes later there was a thunderous explosion, and when Frank looked through the binoculars again, the raft was a ball of fire, flying apart above the waves.

When the smoke and debris settled, Frank studied the water in horror. Joe was gone.

Chapter

9

"JOE!" FRANK SCREAMED, starting for the edge of the cliff. Two MPs grabbed him and dragged him back.

"Take them both to the guardhouse," Captain Hammond commanded, pointing to Frank and Chavo. "I want some questions answered."

"Joe!" Frank screamed again, still struggling as he was pulled to the jeep. It was no use. The guards had him in an unbreakable grip, and he was shoved roughly into the jeep's backseat as Chavo quietly took the seat next to him.

"Stay there and be quiet," an MP growled. The guards climbed into the front seat and started up the jeep.

"I'll get him," Frank muttered as they sped through the base. "I'll get the Director if it's the last thing I do."

"Didn't I tell you to keep quiet?" the MP barked.

Chavo raised a finger to his lips, signaling Frank to stay silent. With his other hand he jabbed a finger three times at the MPs and nodded slowly to Frank.

After a long moment Frank nodded back. This was their only chance, he realized. Chavo held out three fingers and started flashing the count.

On the third count, Frank and Chavo jumped into action, clipping both MPs on the back of the neck. The men pitched forward, unconscious.

Chavo stood and reached over the driver, grabbed the steering wheel, and switched off the ignition. The jeep rolled on even after the power had been cut, sideswiped a hut in a shower of sparks, and then slowed to a halt. Frank and Chavo pulled the MPs out and propped them against the hut.

"They'll be all right when they wake up," Chavo said. He climbed behind the steering wheel.

"Let's get out of here," Frank said, seated in the passenger seat.

They sped for the main gate. The MP there

stepped into their path, his rifle ready. "Stop!" he yelled. He dived to one side, though, as the jeep zoomed past him and smashed through the gate.

Once outside, Frank and Chavo scrambled to Chavo's car. As the MP started firing at them, the car roared off into the night.

"Now what?" Frank asked.

"We dump this car," Chavo said. "The police will be looking for it, and for us. I'll leave you in San Diego and rent a new car."

"Forget that," said Frank. "Where you go, I go. Where are we going?"

Chavo gave Frank a long look, then said, "Tijuana."

Joe woke on the floor of Charity's speedboat and wondered what he was doing there. Then it all came back to him.

He had jumped from the raft just as the night exploded in a shower of flames. But the shock waves that had pushed the still speedboat away from the scene of the blast had tossed Joe down, and he smashed his head on the wooden deck.

How long had he been out? he wondered, and decided it had been only a few seconds. Charity hadn't started the motor yet. Joe stared at the thick column of black smoke that was all that remained of the rubber raft.

"That could have been me," he said, trembling slightly as the realization caught up with him.

Charity looked at him oddly, as if surprised to see him moving. "It wasn't."

"Thanks to you," Joe replied. "Where did you get the boat?"

Charity smoothed her hair. "I borrowed it from the U.S. Navy. I figured it might come in handy."

"And here I thought you'd run out on me."

"Joe, I had to do something. They found out who you really are," Charity said.

Joe frowned. "How?"

"Well," Charity said, flashing her cat smile, "I told the Director."

"I knew it!" Joe raged. "I knew it!"

"Calm down," said Charity. She took a deep breath. "It's time I told you everything."

Joe fumed but said nothing. He stared at the misty sky and waited skeptically for her explanation.

"Oh, don't look like that," she said. "I *had* to turn you in, to establish my credibility."

"Sure. Your credibility. I suppose you stole the Star of Ishtar to establish your credibility."

"As a matter of fact, I did." She pulled a small wallet from her pocket, flipped it open, and held it up where Joe could see. "I'm a federal agent."

Joe read the card without interest. "No, you're not. You're a thief. This is another one of your tricks."

Charity shrugged and put the wallet away. "I know you have no reason to believe me, but I'm telling you the truth. I'm an undercover agent. I've worked for years at establishing a reputation as a master thief. It's the sort of rep that comes in handy when you're dealing with crooks."

"You were sure operating as a thief when we met you in San Francisco," Joe said, his voice still full of doubt.

"Whom did I steal from in San Francisco?" she asked.

"That was government property."

"Right," she said. "I work for the government. They set up things for me to steal, and I steal them. Then I give them back."

Nothing changed on Joe's face to indicate he believed a word she said.

"Don't look at me like that, Joe. I'm telling the truth. You could check it out yourself if we were going back to land, but we have to catch up to that cabin cruiser."

"The government didn't own the Star of Ishtar. Thanks to you, a friend of ours has his reputation and maybe his freedom on the line."

Charity lowered her eyes as if ashamed. "Yes, that's true. But I had to steal it. The

Director gave each of us an assignment to prove we were qualified to take part in his caper. I had to steal the Star and give it to him, but we'll get it back when we capture him.''

She looked at Joe. "When I realized you and Frank lived in Bayport, I knew I could bring you into it. I needed you for backup. Why do you think I made sure you had a trail to follow? Everything's going to work out fine. Trust me.''

Frank's name stirred up Joe's anger all over again. He had, for a second, forgotten about his brother. I shouldn't trust her, he told himself, but she's the only one who can lead me to the Director and Chavo, and she might be on the level. If he was going to get his revenge, he'd have to go along.

"What was the Kid's assignment?''

"Pretty impressive," Charity replied. "He managed to get into the Soviet Historical Institute and get out of Russia with some of the czar's crown jewels. Not all of them, but enough to convince the Director he had what it took.''

"So who's the Director?" Joe asked.

"I don't know. It's my mission to find out. He stays away from everyone, communicating only by television or radio.''

"What's he up to?''

Charity dug under her seat and came back with a map of North America.

"Ever hear of Puerto de Oro?" she asked.

Joe thought briefly. The name was very familiar. "It's an island somewhere off the coast near Tijuana, isn't it?"

Charity nodded. "It's been billed as the perfect paradise. It's become quite a jet-set hangout. Tropical weather, gambling casinos, great beaches. A combination of Monte Carlo and Acapulco."

"The Director's going to knock over a casino?"

"You're thinking too small," Charity said, shaking her head. "He's planning to knock over *the whole island.*"

"Impossible!" Joe answered.

"Hardly," she continued, undaunted. "It's high season for the resort, but the nights are cooling off, so almost everyone stays inside then. The place has a token force of security guards, but there aren't any other real police on the island."

"And with that gas we stole from the navy tonight, the Director can knock the whole place out," Joe said, beginning to put it all together.

"You've got it," Charity said. "Cash, jewels, gold, all kinds of riches. They'll be just lying there for the taking."

Joe heard the engine of another boat and saw a dark mass ahead of them. "There's the cabin cruiser. Let's get them."

"That might be a little hard," Charity said. "They're turning."

It was true. The larger craft was circling around, until it was aimed back at them.

"It's going to ram us!" Charity warned. She spun the steering wheel and shifted gears.

The speedboat sputtered and came to a dead stop.

"What's the matter?" Joe said urgently. The cruiser bore down on them.

Charity turned the ignition, which made a sickly grinding noise. "It's stalled," she said. "But I think I can get it started."

Before Joe or Charity could move, the cabin cruiser plowed into the side of the speedboat. When the larger craft resumed its course to Puerto de Oro, it left nothing but scrap metal and driftwood in its trail.

Chapter

10

"GET OUT OF the car," Chavo said.

Frank Hardy, fueled by a thirst for revenge against his brother's killers, shook off his exhaustion. He was seated in the new car that Chavo had rented. They were stopped dead in traffic, with a long line of cars in front of them. In the distance Frank could see the bright lights of the Tijuana border station. "What's going on?"

"There's usually no trouble getting from the United States to Mexico," said Chavo. "Something's up. They're checking cars."

"Maybe they're looking for someone."

"Like us," Chavo agreed. "Time for another plan."

As car horns behind them began to honk,

Chavo pulled the car to the curb and parked it. Quietly he and Frank left the car and under cover of darkness stole toward the footbridge that ran across the border. There was little traffic on the footbridge, and Frank could see most of the customs officers over at the auto entrance. There was only one guard on the footbridge.

"Be nonchalant," Chavo warned him. "If you're not nervous as you walk past the officer, he'll pay no attention to you."

Frank nodded and walked ahead by a few feet. The officer was standing, reading a magazine. Apparently he wasn't noticing anything at all. As Frank passed him, he glanced up and smiled as if by rote. "Welcome to Mexico, senor," the officer said. "Have a good time."

"Thank you," Frank said, and walked on.

Chavo came up behind, and again the officer smiled. But now there was a cleverness in the grin. Chavo returned the grin, but as he passed the officer, he heard, *"Buenas noches,* Senor Chavo."

Chavo spun to swing at the officer, but the officer grabbed his wrist and twisted it behind his back. "How is the most famous criminal in all of Mexico tonight? We have heard much of you from our neighbors to the north."

"Frank!" Chavo called.

Frank had no choice. He whipped around,

catching the officer in the ribs with a karate kick. Frank felt as uncomfortable about attacking a policeman as he had about fighting the MPs, but Chavo was his only connection to the Director. As the officer staggered, Chavo turned and drove a fist into his stomach.

The officer flew back and landed, stunned, in the dust.

By now other officers had noticed the scuffling on the footbridge, and Frank saw them running toward them through the darkness. "Come on," Chavo yelled. "It's only a short way to the city."

Together they ran into the night, leaving the policemen behind.

Frank wasn't prepared for Tijuana. It was a thriving city with modern buildings and shops. As they walked down wide, newly paved streets, they passed manufacturing plants, shopping centers, and racetracks.

There was the Avenida Revolución, a bustling avenue of restaurants, nightclubs, and small shops where, even at that time of night, tourists wandered, snapping photographs. But Frank didn't have time to be a tourist. Everywhere he looked, he saw his brother's face, and the only thing on his mind was how to nail the Director.

He also remembered Charity. It was her fault they'd gotten involved in this. Frank promised himself that she, too, should finally pay for her crimes.

"In here," Chavo said as they came to the door of a bar. It was a dingy place. The bar was long, lined with rickety stools, and the rest of the place was a dance floor, where only a few couples moved lazily to Spanish guitar music played by a decades-old jukebox. At the far end of the bar a curtain of beads covered the entrance to another room. Perhaps two dozen men were on the barstools.

"What are we doing here?" Frank asked.

"Trust me," Chavo said. As they walked in, he called out, "Hey! Amigos!"

As one, the men on the stools turned around and stared balefully at Chavo. Silently they fingered their drinks, and several of them pulled large knives from their belts and set them on the bar.

"*El jefe!*" Chavo demanded in a loud voice.

"Do you want us to die?" Frank whispered to Chavo with some exasperation.

The scarred man called out something in Spanish, and the bead curtain swirled aside. A slender man stood there, and as he neared, Frank could see he had a carefully trimmed beard and mustache, and wore a white suit. There was a red handkerchief in the pocket.

At the sight of Chavo, he raised his arms and spread them wide, with a big smile. "Chavo!

Amigo!'' he shouted. Throughout the bar the frowns relaxed and men went back to their drinking. The slender man put an arm around Chavo and hugged him like a long-lost relative.

"Who is this?" Frank said.

Chavo looked at Frank as if he had forgotten he was there. "Where are my manners? Frank, this is Benito. Benito, Frank."

The man called Benito extended a hand and said, "Put 'er there, fellow American."

Frank blinked in surprise and shook his hand. "You're American?"

"Sure am," Benito said, winking at him. "Name's Benny. A Coney Island boy."

"We have no time for this," Chavo said. "Benito, we must get to the waterfront at Las Playas de Tijuana."

"See, Chavo and me, we pulled quite a few jobs together in the old days," Benito continued. "As a matter of fact, I seem to remember you owing me some money, Chavo."

"Not now, Benito—"

Benito snapped his fingers, and five men at the bar stood up. Four brought their knives, and the fifth smashed a bottle to a jagged edge against the bar. Slowly they moved toward Chavo.

"Now," Benito said, "about my money . . ."

Frank jumped Benito and got behind him, wrapping an arm around the slender man's neck. "Put them down," he said to the men with the weapons. He tightened his grip on Benito. "Put them down or I'll break his neck."

Hastily Benito spoke a phrase in Spanish, and the men, their eyes dark and suspicious, turned away and returned to the bar. Chavo laughed.

"Very good, Frank," he said. "As I was saying, Benito, we need transportation."

"Give him all the money in your wallet, Chavo," Frank said.

Chavo blinked as if he didn't understand the words. Then he laughed again. "Good joke, Frank."

But Frank wasn't smiling. "Shut up, Chavo. I've just about had it with you. Now, give him all your money, or whatever you owe him, or we won't get anywhere tonight."

Chavo stared at Frank for almost a minute. Finally he sighed and took from his wallet five one-hundred-dollar bills. "We'll forget the interest?" he said to Benito with a wink.

"Sounds good to me," Benito said, and Frank released his grip on him. "What kind of transportation were you looking for?"

Ten minutes later Frank was sitting in a sidecar on a motorcyle that Chavo steered down the Las Playas road. The motorcycle was a leftover from the Second World War, but

Frank found the sidecar quite comfortable. Chavo hadn't spoken to him since they left the bar. Now the scarred undercover man said, "Never do that to me again."

Frank lolled back in the sidecar, his eyes closed and his arms wrapped around himself to keep out the cool night air. "I'd like to know why everyone down here thinks you're a criminal. Sure you were telling me straight about being a Federale?"

Coldly, Chavo replied, "I built a good cover. The local police and the border guards have no need to know what I really am. Why would I lie to you?"

"I don't know," Frank said. "Maybe you're planning to rip off the Director and keep all the loot for yourself. Maybe you're setting me up to help you."

Moodily Chavo said, "Believe what you will," and didn't speak the rest of the trip.

Las Playas de Tijuana was a seaside community, less built-up and also less congested than Tijuana. It had a tranquility that masked what was happening on the fishing barge moored in the harbor. The motorcyle roared up to the gangplank, and Frank and Chavo got off.

"Who's the kid?" Brady asked Chavo as they walked out to the barge on the plank.

Brady sat at the ship end of the gangplank and greeted them with a pistol on his lap.

"Replacement," Chavo replied. "We lost some men on the navy raid. The Director had me sign this one up."

"I don't like it when plans get changed at the last minute," Brady replied as the barge got under way. "By the way, someone's waiting for you in the hold."

"I'll go down in a minute." Chavo and Frank caught their breath and watched the shore lights wink out as the barge moved away from land.

Finally they left Brady and climbed down the ladder into the ship's hold. Frank followed after Chavo and noticed that as soon as he had passed, Brady flashed a signal to Chrome Lasker, who was standing in the control tower. The barge lurched forward and began chugging out of the harbor. Brady followed Frank into the hold.

As Frank's feet hit the floor, a pair of hands grabbed him, yanking him off his feet. Everest had hold of him, and then red-haired Brady reached the floor and helped. The two of them pinned Frank against a wall.

Catching his breath, Frank saw that Chavo was similarly held. There were several crates in the hold, and two of them were pushed together at the center of the room to form a makeshift table.

At the table was Jolly.

Jolly sat next to a radio that was glowing softly and ran the blade of a knife through a candle flame. "Welcome," came the Director's voice from the radio. "Chavo, you are a disappointment to me. I trusted you.

"My friends inside the government have informed me that you are a Federale. Tell me what you've told them about my plans."

"No," Chavo said.

"We could torture you," the voice from the radio continued. "But you might not crack. Instead, let's torture your young friend. Perhaps you'll talk to spare him pain."

"Only one way to find out," Jolly suggested. He stood up, holding out a red-hot blade. Brady tore Frank's shirt open.

As Frank struggled uselessly, Jolly moved the blade closer and closer to his chest.

Chapter

11

How LONG had he paddled? Joe wondered. It seemed to him that he had been floating for hours. He could no longer tell time. His watch had been smashed in the wreck, and overhead the timeless moon just hung there, not moving. He was far from land now, and the ocean, dark and unchanging, spread out in all directions.

With nothing else to do, Joe thought back to the collision. He remembered grabbing Charity as the impact hurled him from the boat. The next thing he knew, he was struggling against the cold, churning waters of San Diego Bay. With a burst of energy he had sputtered to the surface, gasping for air.

Pulling himself onto a large piece of floating

fiberglass, he looked for Charity. But she was nowhere to be seen.

In the distance Joe spotted the cabin cruiser, speeding southwest across the Pacific. Even with the mist on the ocean, the moon was bright enough to show Joe the men on the cruiser's deck, laughing and pointing back at the wreckage. But before he could wonder if the men had spotted him, something else caught his eye. It was dragging behind the cruiser, hanging off one of the ropes that had once towed a rubber raft. It was flat and shiny, like a piece of glass, and in its center was a dark woman-shaped mass.

Charity!

After his strength had finally returned, he flattened himself on the fiberglass and started to paddle with his hands and feet, like a surfer swimming out to meet a wave. He was going to Puerto de Oro, the Port of Gold, no matter how long it took.

He had a brother to avenge.

Joe didn't know where he was. All around him was nothing but empty ocean. He felt sure that somewhere ahead must be the island of Puerto de Oro, but there were no lights, no sounds, only the silent darkness of the ocean on a moonlit night.

Then small waves beat against the fiberglass,

moving against the waves of the ocean. Joe looked around.

A boat was moving toward him, pushing the water before it. A fishing barge.

"Hey!" Joe yelled as the barge neared. Forgetting how tired he was, he paddled toward the boat. "Hey!"

His voice was lost under the sound of the engine. The barge plunged on with no sign of stopping. He waved, trying to get the attention of the two men who had wandered onto the deck. No one noticed him.

He pressed on, pushed back by a wake that grew stronger the nearer he got to the barge. The boat was so close he could smell the stench of fish that it gave off. There was no longer anyone on the deck, but he kept moving.

Water splashed into his face, almost knocking him off the fiberglass hunk, and he flailed to get a grip on it. His hands caught it, and he pulled himself back up.

The barge was right in front of him, moving in a straight line for him.

On the side of the barge, sticking out at right angles to it, was a series of iron bars leading down to the propeller that drove the boat. They were there so fishermen could climb down to the propeller for repairs, Joe realized. But he had another use for them. As another wave rushed at him, he leapt off the fiberglass and dived over the wave, splashing into the water behind it. For a second he was in still water, and he swam as hard as he could for the barge.

Another wave hit him, and he rolled to his side to slice through it with his body. He was almost to the barge. He reached out, fingers grasping for the lowest rung on the ladder of iron bars. They struck air, and he fell back.

If I can't go this way, Joe decided, there's only one thing I can do.

Taking a big gulp of air, he forced himself up as high as he could go, until he was straight up in the water. Then he plunged down, dropping like a stone into the inky depths of the ocean. There, he knew, there were no waves. It was his only chance to get near the barge.

Joe's mouth filled with water, but he forced himself not to breathe or swallow. The barge blotted out a lot of the moonlight, and he couldn't see what he was doing very well, but he managed to stay under the side of the barge, feeling along the edge with his hands.

But then something grabbed his legs and quickly pulled him toward the back of the barge. There the moonlight glistened, and he could see the flash of the propeller blade as it whirled. Joe realized suddenly he was caught in the undertow. It was steadily pulling him straight into the propeller.

Panicked, he swam, but the undertow had him. It came to him in a flash that he wanted to be back by the propeller. Joe stopped struggling and let the undertow pull him back.

As his feet inched closer and closer to the whirling blade, he reached around the side of the barge. His fingers finally locked around an iron bar.

Slowly Joe pulled himself free of the undertow. His head broke the surface of the water, and he took a deep, cool breath of air. As it hit his throat, he choked and coughed up seawater, but the next breath brought clear, sweet air.

Joe climbed the bars and rolled into the barge, landing in a pile of nets that had been stored there. He lay there laughing quietly to himself and staring up at the stars.

"I made it," he announced triumphantly.

Finally he sat up and looked around. The deck was empty. He recognized the kind of boat he was on. It wasn't the type of fishing craft that gets taken out by sportsmen for a long weekend. Professional fishermen who used barges like these usually went out early in the morning and were back at sundown.

What, he wondered, was this barge doing out in the middle of the night with no crew?

Just then, from below, he heard the muffled sound of a radio. It sounded like a man's voice coming from it, but Joe couldn't be sure. He wanted no one to know he was on board until he could check it out.

Crouching, he peered into the captain's tower. It was more of a little room set on top of the deck than a tower. A man stood there, steering the boat, and slowly Joe crept around the edge of the deck for a better look at him.

"Oh, no," Joe gasped as he saw the man's face.

Chrome Lasker stood behind the wheel in the captain's tower.

Joe scrambled out of sight. He had to think. If Lasker was steering the boat, then the boat was being used by the Director, probably on its way to Puerto de Oro.

Anyone else who was on the boat must be in the hold, Joe concluded. If he could capture the boat, he could bring the Director's schemes to a halt.

He crawled on his stomach across the deck, moving toward the hole cut into the deck that led down to the hold. Now he could hear more voices, and these not from a radio. But he couldn't make out what they were saying. He raised himself into a low crouch, checking to see that Lasker hadn't spotted him. Then he reached out for the hold cover.

Joe slammed it shut as muffled cries erupted from below. He grabbed a nearby fishing rod that had been carelessly abandoned on the deck and jammed the handle into the latch, locking the latch in place. No matter how hard they pounded, he knew pounding wouldn't get them out.

Joe sprang to his feet and raced for the door of the captain's tower. He sprinted up the two stairs and hurled himself against the door, hoping to take Lasker by surprise.

But the door was unlatched, and Joe tumbled in, his feet slipping out from under him. Before he could get up, Lasker had pressed a heel against Joe's Adam's apple, pinning him down. The bald-headed villain had drawn and was aiming a gun right between Joe's eyes.

"Well, well. The Kid," Lasker said in surprise. "Good to see you again."

He gave Joe a lopsided smirk. "Too bad you had to come this far to die."

Chapter

12

"WAIT," said the voice from the radio.

Jolly lowered the knife, frowning as he glanced at the radio.

When he finally answered the voice, he meekly said, "Yes, sir?"

But Frank saw contempt in Jolly's eyes as he looked at the radio and his fellow crooks. Scanning the room, Frank saw the contempt on every face there. It occurred to him that, given half a chance, each of them would turn on the others and walk off with all the loot. He filed the insight away, in the hope that he would have a chance to use it.

The radio came alive again. "Let's give Chavo one last chance to come clean, now that he understands the gravity of the situation."

One of the men holding Chavo landed a fist in Chavo's stomach, and the Mexican dropped to his knees, gasping. Another man lifted up Chavo's head.

"Talk," the man said.

Chavo curled his lip into a sneer.

"No go," Jolly told the radio. "Now can I cut?"

"By all means," the radio said. "Be my guest."

Jolly lifted the candle and ran the knife blade up and down the flame. "You know," he told Frank as he approached, "if a knife is hot enough, any wound that it opens will burn shut." Jolly spat on the end of the blade, and Frank heard a quick sizzle. "Unfortunately for you, my young friend, a mere candle will never make a blade that hot."

He stabbed the knife at Frank's bare chest.

As the blade moved, Brady and Everest flinched, and for just an instant Frank felt their grips loosen. Before they could react, he kicked out, catching Jolly in the elbow.

Jolly howled, and the knife flew out of his hand. At the same time, Frank threw his arms straight up in the air, and dropped, using his weight to pull himself out of the grip of Brady and Everest. As he dropped, he grabbed their collars, and they jerked forward. Their heads smacked together with a loud thud.

Frank let go and rolled, knocking Jolly's feet out from under him. The heavyset man, still smarting from the kick in the elbow, collapsed to the floor of the hold.

Then Chavo hurled himself backward, dragging his captors off balance. He rolled into a backward somersault and was free. He sprang to his feet, driving an uppercut into the jaw of the man closest to him.

Frank drove a right hook into the other—and both men fell.

Brady and Everest were already scrambling to their feet, murder in their eyes. Jolly crawled along the floor, frantically trying to find his blade.

Frank rushed forward, head down, and caught Brady in a football tackle, shoving him back against the wall. As they broke apart, Frank clamped his hands together and drove a two-fisted smash into Brady's jaw. The criminal sagged and slid down the wall. He was too dazed to react to anything.

In the meantime Chavo had grabbed Everest around the leg and shoulder and, as the man sputtered in disbelief, lifted him up in the air. Then Chavo lurched forward, body-slamming Everest to the floor. Everest flattened out.

"Pretty impressive," Frank said.

"I watch a lot of wrestling on television," Chavo replied.

Jolly shook the fog from his eyes and lurched to his feet. He waved his knife in front of him as he faced Chavo and Frank. But the heavyset man's confidence was gone.

"Should we flip a coin to see who gets to take the knife away from him?" Frank asked.

With a feeble grin, Jolly flipped the knife around and handed it to Frank hilt-first. "I believe I'm outnumbered."

Chavo tapped his knuckles against Jolly's jaw, and the heavyset man gave out a soft cry, more of surprise than of pain, before he fainted. Frank folded the knife and put it in his pocket.

From above there was a sudden banging sound, as the hold hatch was slammed down.

"They're locking us in," Frank said. He raced up the ladder and started pounding on the hatch cover, but it was no use. Someone had bolted it in place.

"Who?" Chavo asked. "Everyone's down here except Chrome, and he's steering the ship. Who could have put that hatch cover in place?"

"Beats me," Frank said. He eyed the men sprawled unconscious throughout the hold. "I'm more worried about them. When they wake up, they're going to want our hides. We sort of took them by surprise, and I don't think that's going to happen again.

"*Sí,*" Chavo agreed. He began to tear open crates. "We must get that hatch open or find something to tie them with. Help me."

Feverishly Frank and Chavo pulled open crates. There was nothing in them that would help their situation. "What'd you find?" Frank asked.

"One of the crates is filled with guns, another with gas masks." Chavo paused, stroking his chin and staring thoughtfully at nothing. "Gas masks. I begin to understand."

As Chavo grabbed two masks from the crate, Frank pulled out a pouch-size plastic wad. "Look at this. Inflatable life raft." He lifted two small plastic oars from the same crate. "If we ever get out of here, we can use this to get off the boat."

"We will not get out," Chavo said. Already, Brady was beginning to stir. "We need a lever to pry the hatch open."

"Why didn't I think of that?" Frank asked, and leaned back against a crate. It slid away from him, and he turned to see why. The box had been resting on something, and when he pushed against it, it rolled off. The metal something was a crowbar—probably there to pry open the crates.

"Will this do?"

Chavo grinned and dashed up the ladder. He jammed the bar into the small space between the hatch cover and the deck, and with all his strength, using his weight for leverage, Chavo strained at it.

"Hurry!" Frank shouted, picking up the life raft. Brady was on his feet, and the others were moving and groaning. Chavo also groaned as he strained, but the hatch cover stayed in place.

Brady staggered forward, almost blindly, and grabbed at Frank. Frank kicked him away, and the man staggered back to sit again.

"Almost!" Chavo said. He squinted and strained with the effort. The hatch budged.

It flew open all of a sudden, almost knocking Chavo off the ladder.

They emerged onto the deck, tensed and ready for action. There was no one there. Where was the person who had locked them in? Frank's eyes drifted toward the captain's tower, where Chrome Lasker was standing, talking with someone.

Frank shook his head and rubbed his eyes. He was imagining things. The man in the captain's tower with Lasker looked like Joe.

"Jump," Chavo ordered. They could hear the others stirring down below. Chavo leapt over the railing, and Frank followed, pulling the inflation cord on the life raft. It expanded as he fell.

They splashed into the water, and he and

Chavo pulled themselves into the life raft and began paddling away from the barge.

To the west, Frank could see the lights of the island of Puerto de Oro. It shimmered on the sea like a giant jewel, a fantasyland unaware of what was coming to it. All the lights reminded him of Fourth of July fireworks, and he imagined that he could hear the loud popping.

They're shooting at us, he realized.

He crouched down, making himself less of a target, and paddled harder until they were out of sight. The moon had cooperated and was now hidden behind a heavy cloud cover.

"It's good to see you, too, Lasker," Joe said.

Lasker laughed at his joke and tossed the gun on the control panel. Then he took his foot away from Joe's throat, and offered him a hand to help Joe to his feet. "Why are you crashing into my control room, Kid? I thought you were on the other end of the mission."

"I was," Joe explained, half-telling the truth. "In all the action on the other ship, I got thrown overboard. I drifted for a long time, until I spotted this ship, and I climbed aboard. I figured I'd capture it and get to Puerto de Oro that way. How did I know it belonged to the Director?"

"Well, you know now," Lasker said. "Some people are just born lucky, Kid."

As Joe stood, movement outside the window caught his eye. Someone had leapt over the side of the railing. "There's something going on down there." Then in a minute he saw the others, gathered at the railing, shooting into the ocean. Almost as one, they turned and raced to the captain's tower.

"Trouble," Jolly began to tell Lasker. He spotted Joe, and a pleased smile crossed his face. "Kid! Where did you come from?"

"What's the problem?" Lasker asked.

"Chavo has escaped." To Joe he explained, "He double-crossed us. And now he's escaping. We can't see his raft anymore, and our guns won't shoot far enough."

Lasker gave a big belly laugh and reached under the control panel. He pulled out a pair of night binoculars and a flare gun. "Let him escape this. This baby's got a range on it you wouldn't believe, and the flare on it'll burn that raft right off the sea."

"Chavo," Joe muttered, and again he pictured his brother being shot by the Mexican. He grabbed the flare gun.

"That direction, Kid," Jolly said, and he raised the special binoculars to Joe's eyes. Joe could make out a life raft, barely visible against

101

the ocean. A man was in it. Yes, it was Chavo, all right.

Chavo, the man who had killed his brother. Joe knew this might be his only chance to make his brother's murderer pay for that crime.

Carefully he took aim at the raft.

Chapter

13

WHAT AM I DOING? Joe thought with a jolt just before he pulled the trigger. He was about to kill a man, and killing wasn't his style. He wanted to bring Chavo to justice, *real* justice.

That's what Frank would have wanted, he told himself.

He lowered the nose of the flare gun as he fired. An arc of flame shot across the night and exploded in fire and smoke on the ocean. In the blaze, he could no longer see the tiny life raft.

Jolly raised the binoculars to his eyes. "As near as I can tell, a perfect hit." He set them down and patted Joe's shoulder while the others cheered. "Welcome back, Kid. Now we've got to prepare for the main event. The world, as they say, is ours.''

Something burst on the ocean.

Frank raised his head in alarm, to see that the sea was on fire just behind the raft. ''What was that?'' he asked.

Chavo ignored it. ''Flare. We were the target. Let's use it to our advantage, as cover for an escape.'' He took one of the oars from Frank and began paddling. ''So that's how he's going to do it.''

''You mean the Director? You've figured out the caper?''

''Sí,'' said Chavo. ''Puerto de Oro is a self-contained island. It has few police and few buildings. If one were to take, say, the gas stolen from the naval base, and flood the buildings with it, then—''

''Then once you've knocked everyone out, you could wander through the buildings at will and take whatever you wanted,'' Frank continued. ''Everyone would be dead. No witnesses.''

''And they'll have plenty of time to leave the island without anyone contacting the mainland police. It's the perfect crime.''

''Good thing you waited to figure this out until there's no possibility we can get help,'' Frank said with more than a hint of sarcasm.

"I'd hate to think we might need some backup to invade an island that's entirely cut off from the outside world and might be controlled by criminals."

"When we reach Puerto de Oro," said Chavo, "there I will get help."

"Chavo," Frank asked, "can I ask you a question?"

"Go ahead."

"Are you really a cop, or what?"

A burst of laughter erupted from the Mexican, and he said nothing else the rest of the way.

"Welcome to Puerto de Oro," Chavo said as they stepped onto the land ahead of the group on the barge. They had left the life raft in a massive harbor filled with private yachts and walked the rest of the way to the beach. Frank marveled at the sight of casinos and hotels styled like medieval castles, yet gleaming white, even at night. Electric lights made the streets of Puerto de Oro almost as bright as day.

But there was no one on the streets.

"This way," Chavo said, motioning down a street. "We must reach the police station and warn them. There's a radio, too. Men are waiting on the mainland for my orders."

As he ran, Frank's feet slid and skidded

across cobblestones moistened by the sea air. Which men did Chavo mean? Was he really going to call the Federales, or did he have some gang of his own stashed in Tijuana, waiting to come and horn in on the Director's master plan?

Frank resolved he would not turn his back on Chavo until he had the answer.

The police station was plainer than the other buildings, a simple box of stucco and stone. There were bars on all the windows. From inside came the tinny sounds of a mariachi band, played either on an old record player or a cheap radio. It seemed as peaceful and quaint as the rest of the island.

Chavo knocked on the door, yelling something in Spanish. From inside, a voice yelled, *"Qué desea usted?"* Chavo shook his head.

"He asked us what we want," Chavo said.

Frank pushed past him. "Your problem is that this is a resort that caters to rich Americans. Let me give it a try." He pounded on the door, shouting, "Help! Robbery!" Frank looked at Chavo. "How do you say 'I want to report a theft'?"

"Quiero denunciar un robo," Chavo replied.

"Quiero denunciar un robo," Frank repeated, pounding again at the door.

Finally the door opened a crack and a single brown eye peered out. "Come back tomorrow," a Hispanic voice called. "We cannot help you now."

Chavo hurled himself into the door, shoving it open. The figure at the door fell backward, and Frank and Chavo pushed their way in.

Frank helped the man on the floor to his feet. He was in his twenties, scrawny, and dressed in the uniform of a Mexican police deputy. Quickly he pulled his hand away from Frank and nervously brushed some dust off his khakis. In the meantime Chavo began to rummage frantically through the office. It was as small as it looked from outside, but it was packed with file cabinets. Next to the main desk was a teletypewriter. Chavo ripped pages from the teletypewriter, scanned them, and scowled.

"The radio," he insisted. "Where is your radio?" When the deputy refused to answer, Chavo stormed into the next room, toward the jail.

Frank expected the deputy to be angry about the break-in, but instead there was nothing but fear in his eyes. Those eyes weren't focused on Frank, but on the room that Chavo had just entered. He wondered why the deputy was so uneasy. There could be only one reason.

"Chavo!" Frank yelled as he flung the deputy aside. "It's a trap." He sprinted toward the door, but a man appeared in his way. The man was dressed in a white suit. A thick mustache adorned his upper lip, and grim mirth danced in the man's black, ratlike eyes.

It was Cat Willeford.

"Come in," he said, waving a gun at Frank. He motioned to the deputy. "You too."

"You won't shoot us," Frank said. "You'd bring the whole island down on you."

Willeford raised the pistol and fired at the ceiling. Powdered plaster rained down like a dust storm as the deafening roar echoed through the police station.

"Coming?" Willeford asked, and Frank and the deputy filed past him to the jail area.

Two others of the gang were also in there, tossing an unconscious Chavo into a cell. "Too bad," said Willeford. "I had to quiet him down." He flagged Frank and the deputy into the cell and slammed the door.

In the next cell Frank saw the chief of police and another deputy. He assumed that was all the law on the island.

"You're going to leave us here?" he asked Willeford.

"Not quite," the rat-eyed man answered before he vanished with his cronies into the outer office. Willeford returned a moment later, wearing a gas mask and holding a canister. He lifted up the mask. "Pleasant dreams." It sounded like a farewell.

Then he slipped the mask back on and crouched down. With a flip of his thumb he knocked open the valve on the canister. A white gas began spraying into the police station.

With a cheerful motion, Willeford dropped the cell-door keys on the floor outside Frank's cell, and then left.

As soon as the door closed, Frank was on his stomach, reaching through the bars. He stretched to grab the keys, but Willeford had dropped them just outside his reach. They lay there, tantalizing him, as the white cloud filled the room.

Coughing, his eyes stinging from the gas, Frank slapped Chavo. He wouldn't wake up. Frank slapped him again. Finally, the cell blurring before his eyes as the gas threatened to overcome him, Frank clamped a hand over Chavo's mouth and pinched his nose shut.

Chavo gasped awake, choking from the lack of air to his lungs. Before Frank could explain, he sized up the situation. The police chief and the deputies were flat on the floor, trying to reach the keys.

Chavo gave it a try and failed. He started to stand up, and then he sniffed at the gas. His eyes widened in terror, and he dropped back to his knees. Frank thought he looked sick.

"Knockout gas?" Frank asked, but he saw by the look in Chavo's eyes it wasn't so.

"Poison gas," Chavo replied weakly. "To kill us."

He threw himself against the bars, straining for the keys just out of reach as the cloud of death descended. Chavo slumped and shook his head. "It's no use."

They were trapped.

Chapter

14

FRANK PEELED OFF his shirt, holding it over his nose and mouth. Chavo ordered the others to stay down, breathing the air that remained under the thickening cloud. But Frank knew the dense gas would eventually force all the air out of the building. He had to reach the keys.

He got on his stomach again and stretched for the keys. Three inches, he thought. If only his arm would stretch three more inches!

He rolled onto his back, gasping for air. The gas stung his nostrils, choking him. He flattened against the floor, trying to stay beneath the cloud.

Something hit against his leg. Frank patted the floor with his hand, but there was nothing under his leg. He reached into his pocket.

There, forgotten, was the knife he had taken from Jolly on the barge.

Quickly he flicked the knife blade and stretched out again. The tip of the knife touched the edge of the key ring. He pulled it toward him. The knife blade slipped away. He tried again, slipping the blade under the ring this time. Slowly, so slowly Frank felt as if he wasn't moving at all, he lifted the knife, catching the ring.

The key ring slid down the length of the knife until it was in Frank's hand.

He pressed his face to the floor as far as he could, took one last breath, and stood up. As long as I don't breathe in, Frank thought, it won't get me. The thing that worried him was how long he would be able to hold his breath.

Frank worked the keys in the lock until the jail door swung open. He could see nothing but the white cloud. His ears and eyes stung as he staggered to the canister, but he held his breath as he tried to close the valve.

Willeford had broken it.

He lifted the canister, and the effort made him exhale, then inhale, without meaning to. Gas rushed into his lungs, and he felt himself weakening. With a loud cry, he lunged forward, into the front office, and smashed the canister through a window.

The bars stopped the canister, bouncing it

back into Frank's arms, but the window shattered. The rush of cool air cleared his head. Frank opened the front door to let in more air.

Standing outside on the steps was one of the men who had been with Willeford in the jail. Like Willeford, he now wore a gas mask. The gun he held was aimed at Frank.

Frank swung the canister like a baseball bat. It slammed into the side of the man's head, knocking him flat. Frank let go of the canister and fell to his knees next to the gunman, ripping at the thug's mask.

In seconds Frank had it on his own face. Then he rushed back into the deadly cloud in the jailhouse and, one by one, dragged the others to safety.

He sat on the ground in front of the police station, catching his breath as the others recovered. Finally he had the energy to remove the gas mask. He decided not to let it out of his sight. It might come in handy, now that the Director's scheme was in motion. Chavo entered a heated conversation in Spanish with the police chief, and when it was over he grabbed Frank by the arm and pulled him to his feet.

"The first thing Willeford did was smash the chief's radio," Chavo said. "We have one other chance." He jerked his head in the direction of the main hotel. "Brendan Buchanan, who owns the big casino on the island, has a two-way radio in his office."

Frank flashed Chavo a cocky grin. "Then we'd better get there before someone destroys that one too."

They moved stealthily and kept low. Frank noticed activity down by the docks. They crept closer for a better look, staying in the shadows.

The fishing barge was in, and the Director's gang was marching away from it. Each of them carried a large bag, and each wore a gas mask. The seven men marched toward the hotel.

"Seven?" Frank whispered to Chavo. "Where did they get a seventh from? There were only six on the boat."

"Don't forget the one who closed the hatch." Chavo watched grimly as the men blocked their path to the hotel. "We are beaten. There are too many of them, and we cannot get past them without them seeing us."

"Stay here," Frank said. "I've got an idea."

He slipped on the gas mask to conceal his identity and ran up to the line of criminals, trying not to make any noise. Without a sound, he slipped an arm around the neck of the last man in line, dragging him back. The man struggled, but the mask muffled his cry.

Chavo jumped up, ripped the man's gas mask off, and knocked him out. He slipped the mask on as Frank took the man's belt off and bound him with it.

"Perfect," Frank said, eyeing the masked Chavo. "You look like a master criminal again."

The hotel was filled with a bright pink gas that wafted in streams around Frank and Chavo as they entered. Elegantly dressed people littered the hotel lobby and stairs, an eerie stillness clutching their fallen bodies. Men in gas masks moved, taking watches, jewelry, and wallets from them and dropping the items in their bags.

They're breathing, Frank realized, relieved that here, at least, the thieves had not used poison gas.

They started up the stairs, and for a moment Chavo paused, looking back. Frank saw his eyes narrow. "What's the matter?"

"The seventh man from the dock," Chavo said. "The one we couldn't identify. I thought I saw him in the corner of my eye. I was mistaken."

They continued up. More bodies were on the stairs, lying where they'd fallen when the gas hit. From above them came the cry, "It's about time you got here. Let's go. The top floor hasn't been touched."

It was Everest. For a moment Frank froze,

sure they'd been spotted. Then he remembered the masks. Everest couldn't see who they were.

Chavo nodded, and Everest vanished back up the stairs.

"Let's go," Frank said. "According to the guide we passed on our way in, the manager's office is on the top floor."

They stopped on a balcony and looked at the activity below. The balcony opened out over a large casino, and masked figures scurried from table to table, robbing the gamblers and looting the money on the tables. For the first time, Frank fully understood just how big this crime really was.

He and Chavo continued up the stairs. Here and there men in gas masks popped in and out of hotel rooms. "There are more here than I recruited," Chavo said. "The Director must have had other scouts over here already in place."

"For a job like this, I can understand that," Frank replied. They reached the top of the stairs. On this floor there were no guest rooms, only offices. Frank went from door to door, until he found a plaque that read Manager.

"Here it is," he called to Chavo.

Gingerly he turned the knob. The unlocked door swung open.

The room was dark, and they dared not turn

on a light. Wisps of pink gas hung in the air, but it smelled sweeter than the air downstairs. Against the back window, which overlooked the harbor, was an antique desk.

A man sprawled with his face on the desk. Frank raised the man's hand, and it dropped back to the desk without pause. "Unconscious," Frank said. "I assume this is the manager."

"Never mind him," Chavo said. "Find the radio." He pulled books off the shelves and knocked open file drawers.

There was no sign of a radio.

"It's got to be here somewhere," Chavo insisted. He scratched his head. "Maybe it's one of those new miniaturized jobs. He could have it in his desk."

Frank stepped behind the desk and gently moved the unconscious manager to one side. He pulled open the desk drawers and rifled though them. Only papers. Exasperated, he slammed the top drawer shut.

His knuckle brushed against a button underneath the lip of the desktop. Curious, he pressed it.

A bookcase swung away from the wall, revealing a small room inside.

"The radio!" Chavo exclaimed, and rushed into the room. In seconds he was working the controls of the shortwave, repeating into the microphone, "Mayday! Mayday! Please acknowledge."

Frank stepped in, studying the hidden room. Why would a hotel manager install one? he wondered. He pressed his hand against the smooth white wall, and it gave way. As he heard Chavo speaking to the mainland police, he said, "I think we have a problem."

Behind the second wall was a small television studio.

"You do have a problem," the hotel manager agreed. He stood outside the door, very much awake, a pistol in his hand. "Yes," he said in answer to the shocked looks on their faces, "I am the hotel manager and owner."

Frank studied the man's face. There was something strangely familiar about him, though Frank was certain he hadn't seen him before. Under the man's nose, almost invisible, were nose filters. That, Frank realized, was how the manager had kept himself safe from the gas.

The manager gave them a tight smile. "Of course, you may call me the Director."

Chapter

15

WEARING HIS GAS MASK, Joe Hardy strolled through the casino. He had walked off the barge with the others, but since then had not joined them in their activities. He only watched as the criminals stripped Puerto de Oro of its wealth. Across the casino, at the roulette tables, two men were cleaning out the cash.

One crook picked up a diamond necklace and held it up to the light, checking its quality. The thief wiped the lenses on his gas mask with a sleeve, and when he still couldn't see well enough, he slipped the mask off and held the diamonds to the light again.

A satisfied smile crossed the man's lips. On the other side of the room, Joe's blood began to boil.

The man with the diamonds was Cat Wille-ford.

A thick hand clapped down on Joe's shoulder, startling him. He was at the point when he wanted to hit someone who deserved hitting, and his first thought was to spin around and start swinging. He held himself back. Like the others, this guy's face was masked, but Joe couldn't mistake the voice or the shape.

"You'd better do your share, Kid," Jolly said. "We wouldn't want you to miss out on your cut of the take, now, would we?"

"Someone would have to turn me in," Joe replied. "You wouldn't do that."

Jolly sighed. "I might hate to, that's true. But if the money was right . . ."

"What do we do with all this stuff once we get it?"

"Didn't they tell you, Kid? There's a central collection point, a truck out in the town square. We take everything there."

"And?" Joe asked.

"I don't get you."

"How do we get paid? And how's a truck going to help us? This is an island."

"You worry too much," Jolly replied. "The Director wouldn't be dumb enough to run out on us. There are enough guys here who'd be glad to track him to the ends of the earth to make him pay.

"On the other hand . . ." Jolly rubbed the back of his neck, still thinking about Joe's question. "That point about the truck is well-taken. I hope nothing is wrong. I get most unpleasant when someone betrays me."

"Sorry to hear about that," Joe said. Whipping around, he swung up, knocking the gas mask from Jolly's face. His fist landed in the heavyset man's stomach, and Jolly sucked in a lungful of pink gas.

"Kid," Jolly said softly, sadness in his voice. He opened his mouth again, as if to shout, and then dropped to the floor. The gas had taken effect.

Joe glanced around the room. No one had noticed his scene with Jolly. He stashed Jolly under a blackjack table, then picked up the bag of loot Jolly had been carrying. The heavyset man had been right about one thing. Joe would be a lot less conspicuous if he were carrying a bag.

He wanted to stay inconspicuous—he had a lot of scores to settle, starting with Cat Willeford.

A big bag tossed over his shoulder, Willeford left the casino and headed into the dining room next door. Joe followed. None of the others paid any attention to them. And if they found Jolly lying there? Would they raise the alarm?

No, Joe decided. They'd probably rob him of any valuables he had left.

Willeford was in the kitchen when Joe caught up with him. Joe called his name, and the rat-eyed man looked up.

"I've been looking forward to this," Joe said.

"Who are you?" asked Willeford.

Joe lifted his gas mask for a moment, and Willeford smiled. "Kid, you've got almost as many lives as I do."

"The name's not Kid. It's Joe Hardy. You should never have tried to kill me." Joe clenched his fists and took a step toward Willeford. "You're out of lives now, Cat."

Willeford ran. He and Joe left their bags sitting in the kitchen, and Joe chased him into the main hallway. Other criminals watched them as they ran, and Joe could hear them laughing. He knew none of them would lift a hand to help Willeford. They were too interested in their loot.

Joe stopped dead in his tracks as he reached the hallway. Two masked figures were starting up the stairs, and one of them turned his face just enough for Joe to recognize the eyes. He'd never forget those eyes.

That was Chavo, the guy who'd killed his brother. Joe started after Chavo.

Willeford took advantage of Joe's shift of

attention, catching Joe under the chin with his forearm. The blow knocked Joe off his feet and sent him crashing on his back on the floor. Willeford dropped down like a piledriver, smashing both fists into Joe's chest.

Joe tried to shake off the haze that was swallowing him. Somewhere he was dimly aware that Willeford was clawing at his face, trying to slip his mask off. Struggling to keep the mask on, Joe tried to stand. Willeford went for a new hold, wrapping an arm around Joe's head while Joe was still bent over.

Joe stood suddenly, locking one hand under Willeford's shoulder and the other in the man's belt. He kicked backward, and Willeford was in the air as Joe tucked himself into a roll. They both crashed to the floor on their backs.

Willeford hit first, and he hit hard. While the crook thrashed around, trying to pull himself together, Joe punched him again. Willeford stopped moving and lay still.

Joe turned his eyes to the stairs. Now it was Chavo's turn.

"You're robbing your own resort?" Frank said in disbelief.

"Certain financial setbacks make it necessary," the Director said. "Everything was planned, except for the interference from you and your brother."

As the Director spoke to Frank, Chavo inched toward him. The Director calmly turned and pointed the gun at Chavo's heart. "Uh-uh," he said. "Please don't interrupt."

Frank and Chavo stood back as the Director continued.

"Take Mr. Chavo here, a Federale operating undercover as a criminal. He was the perfect tool. I could use him to recruit the people I needed and set up the operation. And he fell right in line, eager to arrest large numbers of crooks in the commission of a crime."

"You knew about Chavo all along?" Frank asked.

"My boy, he's the most important part of my plan. When the Mexican authorities raid this island and capture the army of criminals I've assembled, I won't have to pay any of them. I, and the millions of dollars collected here tonight, will simply disappear."

"That's why you relayed everything through radio or television," Frank said, "and why you appeared fully masked. Why would anyone associate a hotel manager with the mastermind who robbed the place? You're in the clear."

"Except for us," Chavo said tensely. "We know who you are."

The Director picked up a shoebox, pressed a button on it, and slid it across the floor of the secret room. "I was coming to that. The final part of my plan is for my office to be bombed. It's the perfect way to cover my tracks. Of course, it would appear to all as if I'd been killed in the blast—''

"Of course," Frank said.

"Now it seems your bodies will be found in the wreckage. The thief who planted the bomb"— the Director gestured to Frank, then to Chavo—"and the brave policeman who tried to stop him. How tragic."

The Director checked his watch. "Five minutes. I really must be going." He stepped back, and the secret door began to close.

Frank leapt for the Director, but he was too slow. The man swung his gun, cracking Frank on the skull. He fell back, unconscious, but Chavo moved, knocking the Director back before he could pull the trigger. They tumbled together out of the radio room, and the pistol slipped from the Director's grip, skittering across the floor. When they stopped rolling, Chavo was on top of the Director, pinning his arms down.

"It's all over," Chavo said.

But another masked figure appeared from nowhere and slammed the back of Chavo's head. He slumped weakly to the floor. The Director scrambled to his feet, racing out the door as Chavo, clutching his head, looked up.

Joe Hardy stood over him, ready for business. "You killed my brother, you slime."

Beneath the gas mask, Chavo's eyes widened at the sound of Joe's voice. He tried to get to his feet, but Joe held him down. Then Joe grabbed him by the collar and lifted him up, knocking the gas mask from Chavo's face.

Joe planted a punch on Chavo's jaw, and Chavo staggered back but remained on his feet.

"Your brother's alive."

Joe could barely hear Chavo's voice.

"What?" Joe said. He couldn't believe his ears. "You're just saying that to save your skin."

"No. Please. You must listen if you want to save him." Chavo half-raised a hand and pointed to the secret room. "Behind that wall—I was just with him." He took a faltering step forward, dread written all over his face. "He's in there with a bomb."

He's lying, Joe told himself. But there was a look of true panic on Chavo's face, and Joe knew he couldn't pass up even the slightest chance that Frank still lived. He lunged for the secret door.

It was too late. The wall disintegrated from the force of the blast.

He flew back into darkness, hoping against hope that Chavo had been lying about Frank.

Chapter

16

SOMETHING STUNG JOE'S CHEEK. He tried to wave it away, but it stung him again. Finally he opened his eyes a crack—then he parted them wide.

Frank was kneeling over him, gently bringing him around. He saw dark smudges on Frank's face, and his clothes were tattered, but he was alive!

"You're still breathing, brother," Frank said, smiling. "We both made it."

Joe sat up and saw Chavo standing impatiently behind Frank. Frank turned to the Mexican and said, "Go ahead. We'll catch up in a few minutes." As Chavo left, Frank helped Joe to his feet.

"What happened?" Joe asked. "That bomb

knocked me clear across the room. You couldn't have survived if you'd been right on top of it."

"You should have seen all the great electronic equipment in there." Frank laughed. Then his face turned serious. "A fan's dream, all this radio and TV stuff—very bulky. When I realized I couldn't get out of the room, I put the bomb in one end and pushed the equipment to the other."

Joe began to grin. "And you hid behind the equipment when the bomb went off." He shook his head. "It's just like you to leave me to take the worst of it."

"The equipment took the worst. There's not much of it left," Frank said. His face grew grim. "I'm really glad to see you, Joe. I thought you were dead."

"I thought *you* were, too." Joe gave his brother a big hug. "Let's try never to go through that again, okay?"

"Deal," Frank said. "Now let's find Chavo."

When the Hardys caught up to him, Frank asked, "Do you trust us to get the Director while you try to reach the police?"

"I suppose I do not have a choice," Chavo replied with a grin. "I will have to find another working radio at another hotel."

"Good." Frank cocked his head toward the

door and glanced at Joe. "Now, why don't we go round up the Director."

The hotel was empty, except for the still-unconscious guests and staff. Every room had been stripped, every safe-deposit box looted. The Director's plan had worked almost flawlessly.

"Get back," Frank said. They both jumped for the shadows as two criminals, loaded down with bags, walked by. "They'll probably lead us to the Director as well as anyone." Staying out of sight, they followed the two thieves to the town square, where everyone had lined up to pour jewelry and money into an old dump truck.

"A truck?" said Frank.

"Jolly said something about this," Joe explained. "It's supposed to get all this stuff off the island."

"How can a truck get out?" Frank said in disbelief. "It doesn't look very seaworthy."

"That's what we were told," Joe said. "I guess we'll find out soon enough."

"Come on." Frank glanced around. "I've got an idea." Quickly he led Joe to the nearest building. Frank jumped up, catching the fire escape. They climbed up three sets of metal stairs, until they were on a roof overlooking the bizarre scene.

129

They watched for a while.

"Look," Joe said, breaking the silence.

Out on the ocean, a fleet of lights grew brighter and brighter as they approached the island. A high-pitched whine became louder, then softer, then louder still.

"It's the police," Joe said.

"Then Chavo did find another radio." Frank nodded. "But the Director planned on this. Hang on, little brother. I think we're about to catch the ride of our lives."

On the ground, the criminals were reacting to the oncoming sirens. Joe watched in amusement as they frantically pointed out to sea. Several rushed the truck and tried to get into the driver's cabin, but the doors were locked.

"That's not the Director driving," Joe said.

"No, but I bet he'll be where the truck's going," Frank said, watching it careen down the street. "Get ready."

"What are we supposed to do from up here?"

"Jump," said Frank.

"Jump?"

"Jump!"

Together, they leapt.

The Hardys fell three stories, to smash into a lumpy pile of loot. They were in the back of the old dump truck, speeding through Puerto de Oro at a breakneck pace.

As he bounced around on the jewelry and cash, Frank imagined the look on the Director's face when he got to his destination and found them waiting for him.

The truck turned off the street and onto a dirt road, heading for the heart of the island. Far behind were the casinos, criminals, and police. Now the scenery was tropical forest so thick that it was almost jungle, and the road turned to a trail barely wide enough for the vehicle. It looked as if no one had ever lived on this part of the island. It was almost wilderness.

The police would never look for the Director here.

They rode up a mountain, then down the other side. Joe stood and looked out over the hood of the dump truck. The truck was heading toward a small inlet, lit orange and purple by the rising sun. There was a long stretch of beach beside the water, and on the sand, a dark winged object.

"You're not going to believe this," Joe said. "I guess you can get anything from government surplus if you try hard enough."

Frank took a look. "I believe it. It's the only way his plan could work."

The truck rolled onto the beach and into the fuselage of the cargo plane waiting there.

The Hardys lay flat on the loot as the aircraft's engines started one by one. The truck door slammed, and Frank could hear the Director barking orders. The ramp up to the airplane was pulled in, and the entrance bay closed. Then the plane started to move. Frank and Joe began to slide over the loot as the plane rose into the air.

"Frank," Joe began as the plane leveled off, but Frank clapped a hand over Joe's mouth, silencing him. The Director's triumphant laughter echoed in the belly of the plane.

Then came a grinding noise. "Oh, no!" Frank yelled, no longer caring if he were heard or not.

The front of the dump truck began to tip up.

Frank and Joe crawled through the loot, trying to reach what was now becoming the top of the mound, but the farther they crawled forward, the more the slipping pile of riches carried them back. The back gate of the truck opened, the loot spilling onto the floor of the airplane. The Director danced around the pile with joy.

Then he saw the Hardys, and his face changed. "Nick! Charlie!" he called, going for the pistol stuck inside his belt.

Joe dived, tackling him. A shot rang out, ricocheting off the wall of the plane. Then Joe reached the Director, grabbed his gun hand, and tore the pistol from his grip.

"Drop it," a voice snarled. "Hands where we can see them." Joe spun, pistol ready, to find himself facing two unshaven men with automatic rifles. The one who spoke wore a T-shirt, and his black hair was cut close to his head, almost like a skullcap. His gun was aimed straight at Joe. The second gunman trained a rifle on Frank.

Sagging, Joe dropped the pistol and raised his hands.

"This one's no problem, Nick," the other man said as he shoved Frank to Joe's side. The Director picked up his fallen pistol.

"The Hardys," the Director said. "Is there no getting rid of you?"

"Smarter guys than you have tried," Joe answered defiantly.

A slow smile spread over the Director's face. "That may be true. But I'll be the one to succeed." He signaled the two other men, who nudged Frank and Joe toward the bay door.

"Let me introduce Nick and Charlie," the Director went on. "They've had quite a bit of experience with smuggling by air. For instance, do you know what they do with contraband when the police are closing in?"

He hit a switch, and the bay doors opened. Frank and Joe looked out over the dark Pacific, half a mile below.

"We dump it," Nick said with a grin.

The Director grinned back. He pointed to the bay door, then turned to the Hardys. "To have gotten into the truck, you must be good at jumping."

The smugglers cocked their automatic rifles and pressed them in the Hardys' ribs.

"I'd like to see a demonstration," the Director said. "So jump."

Chapter

17

"A HIGH-DIVE COMPETITION is no fun with just two people, Director," a woman's voice said. "Maybe you should join them."

The Director and the Hardys all turned at once, shock on their faces.

"Charity!" Joe yelled.

"Get her!" the Director shouted to the smugglers. Nick just turned where he was, training his rifle on his supposed boss.

Charity stepped from the cockpit. "I don't think your men will follow your orders anymore, Director. I've bought them off."

"Imp-p-ossible." The Director stuttered over the word. "I offered them a cut of the loot! How could you top that?"

Charity shrugged. "I offered them *half* the.

loot. Once we take it from you, of course. Now, if you'd be so kind—'' She waved them toward the open bay door.

"You can't!" Joe said.

She laughed. "True enough." To the Director she said, "Close that door. I've never killed anybody, and I don't want to pick up bad habits."

"Any *more* bad habits?" Joe sneered.

Charity feigned a brokenhearted look. "Why, Joe. And after I just saved your life. How ungentlemanly." She signaled, and the two smugglers shoved the Hardys and the Director into the plane's interior. Charity reached into her pocket, pulling out two pairs of handcuffs.

"Souvenirs from police I've run into," she explained.

The smuggler named Nick opened the driver's door of the dump truck, lowering the window. He stuck Joe on one side of the open door and Frank on the other, holding their hands up. Then Charity snapped the cuffs over their wrists. They were stuck, trapped by the door. The smuggler named Charlie handcuffed the Director to the truck's rear bumper, just out of reach of the loot.

"You lied to me," Joe accused Charity. "You're no government agent."

She began to laugh. "Of course I lied. I'm a thief. It worked out so much better this way."

"I can understand why you wanted to rip off the Director," Frank said, looking back at the loot. "But why bring us into it?"

"The oldest reason in the world, Frank," Charity said. "Misdirection—keeping the enemy off guard. You were the wild cards. While the Director was busy watching you, he couldn't keep an eye on me."

"So you pulled that heist in Bayport just to lure us in." Frank was talking out loud to explain it to himself.

"I think you'll agree it worked out well." She studied Joe's angry scowl. "Or maybe not. We don't have to agree on everything."

The Director sat on the floor, his tear-filled eyes fixed and staring. "How did you know? How did you know?"

"You're going to think this is funny," Charity explained. "I was in Puerto de Oro six months ago, when you were planning this caper. You write everything down, did you know that? It's the sort of thing that will get you in trouble one of these days."

"I destroyed all those notes!" the Director burst out. "No one ever saw them except me."

"And the woman who robbed your safe," Charity added, to the man's surprise. "Me. It was a good plan, but I think mine was better."

The Director sank into silence, his face gray with shame.

"What are you going to do with us?" Frank asked. "You can't let us go. We know too much."

"*What* do you know?" Charity countered. "You don't know who I am or where I'm going. No, you really can't do me much harm at all." She looked wistfully out the window. "We'll be in Guatemala before too long. The plane will land there, we'll take the loot out, and leave you with the plane. How's that?"

"Just great," Joe said sourly.

She patted him gently on the cheek, trying to raise his spirits. "Don't take it like that, Joe. You'll get free pretty quickly. I'll see to that. Then all you have to do is find the Guatemalan police and explain everything to them, and by the time you do that, I'll be long gone.

"It's a shame, really," Charity said, looking at the Hardys. "We made such a good team. Maybe we can work together again someday."

"Over my dead body," Joe muttered.

"Don't say things like that," Charity scolded him. "Someday you'll run into someone who'll take that suggestion seriously."

Like the Director, Joe sank into silence and fumed. He couldn't believe it. Charity had outwitted them again.

The plane dipped, and Frank saw light coming from around the front end of the plane, streaks of bright red. The sun was almost up, but it had risen to the right of them.

She's lying again, he thought to himself. If the sun is to the right, we're flying northeast. That means we're over the United States.

"This is where I get out," Charity said. The plane landed, skidding along a landing strip crudely scratched out of the desert. When the plane came to a halt, Nick opened the bay doors.

A man stood at the bottom of the ramp, half-hidden in the morning grayness. He was short and thin, with thinning dark hair that formed a widow's peak. His thick glasses reflected the lights from inside the plane. Behind him was a rent-a-van, the kind used by millions of people throughout the country. Once they got on the highway with that, Frank knew, the thieves would vanish without a trace.

The man walked up the ramp, into the lit area.

"Renner!" Joe shouted. Forgetting the handcuffs, he lunged for the insurance investigator but jerked back abruptly, stopped by the end of his chain.

Renner frowned. "What are they doing here? This ruins everything. They'll destroy my career."

"You'll be rich, remember?" Charity reminded him. "You won't need a career. Let them be."

Nick went outside and backed the rent-a-van to the cargo-bay doors. A third smuggler, the pilot, came out of the cockpit and, with Renner, Charity, and the others, shoveled the loot into boxes, piling them in the back of the van.

Frank and Joe watched this without comment. The Director, on his knees with one hand cuffed to the truck, desperately scratched and clawed at any loose baubles or money that fell as they were loaded. Laughing, the smugglers let him keep whatever he could grab.

Renner, though, snatched the loot away from the Director and stuffed it into the last box.

When the final box was in the van, Charity blew goodbye kisses to the Hardys. "Thank you, boys," she said. "I couldn't have done it without you." She walked down the ramp out the bay door to the van.

Renner called the smugglers into the cockpit of the plane. There were three dull thuds, and moments later, Renner reappeared alone.

In his hands were two containers of gasoline.

"Charity!" he called pleasantly. "Could you come back here a moment?"

Joe could see her against the spreading morning light. Now that Charity's schemes were finished, it seemed to Joe that all the energy had gone out of her. She yawned with disinterest and started up the ramp again.

Renner pressed his back against the wall next to the bay door and pulled a revolver from under his coat. He cocked the hammer.

"Run!" Joe yelled. "It's a double cross!"

Angrily Renner spun and snapped off a shot at Joe. It hit the driver's mirror on the dump truck and shattered it. Renner leapt onto the ramp. Charity had just reached the van when Renner fired a shot over her head.

"The next one goes in your back, Charity," he said.

Charity stopped. Putting her hands behind her head, she walked back into the plane. Keeping his gun at her back, Renner cuffed her to the Director, wrapping the handcuff chain around the dump truck's back bumper.

"Congratulations," she said to Renner. "You win."

Renner sneered. "But I'm not safe. I won't be, until none of you can threaten me." He went back to the gasoline containers, uncapped them, and splashed gas throughout the plane.

With a theatrical bow, Renner faced the Hardys and Charity. "I want to thank everyone for making me very, very wealthy. I'll never forget you." He hit the bay-door switch and ran outside.

Just before the bay door closed, Renner lit a

match and tossed it back into the plane. The match landed in a pool of gasoline, and in a flash the plane was in flames.

Frank and Joe struggled against the handcuffs as the fire raced toward them, but the chain held. There was nothing they could do.

The plane was going up in smoke, and it would take them with it.

Chapter

18

"JOE, PULL DOWN on your end of the chain," Frank ordered.

Joe dropped to his knees. On the other side of the door, Frank pushed himself through the truck window and somersaulted to his feet on Joe's side of the door.

"Very good. And here I thought I'd have to do *all* your thinking for you," Charity said.

"I supposed you had this planned all along," Joe chided. Charity flashed him a sly grin.

"We haven't got time for clever chatter, Joe," Frank said as the flames grew near. With his free hand he pulled on the bumper holding Charity and the Director down. "We've got to get them out of here. Where's the handcuff key, Charity?"

"Save me," pleaded the Director.

"I'm afraid Renner has the key," Charity said coolly. "But if you'd take that pin off my lapel . . ." Frank undid the gold lapel pin and handed it to her. With her free hand she inserted the sharp point of the pin into the handcuff lock—freeing both herself and the Director.

"Where do you think you're going?" Joe said as Charity bolted for the bay-door control. He grabbed her wrist and pulled her back.

"Nowhere, from the looks of that," she said, pointing out the fire that blocked the exit.

"Get into the back of the truck," Frank ordered Charity and the Director. "Come on, Joe."

The Hardys dashed to the cockpit. The three smugglers sprawled in the pilot seats, unconscious. Joe slapped Nick awake, and as the smuggler woke, the smoke filling the cabin told him the situation. "Help us get your friends out of here," Frank told Nick. "Or you won't get out either."

They dragged the other two to the back of the truck. Fire devoured the cargo bay. Still handcuffed together, Frank and Joe climbed into the driver's cab. Frank started up the engine.

Seconds later, the burning truck smashed through the side of the plane. The truck tumbled to the ground and rolled, spilling its passengers. It took one more tumble, then came to a stop on its side.

Frank and Joe, bruised, crawled out together. They ran across the sand and fell in the flash of heat as fire roared over the truck and plane. Exhausted, Frank sprawled out on the ground.

Joe raised his head. For the first time he realized they were in a desert, and as he watched, Charity and the others spread out and ran off. Joe tried to spring to his feet, but the handcuff pulled him down again. "They're getting away!" Joe said insistently. "We've got to stop them!"

"We don't need to," Frank said, his eyes closed. "Listen."

Overhead there was the familiar *thwipping* of helicopter blades. Three choppers descended in a triangular pattern, and armed police officers leapt out. In seconds the police led Charity, the Director, and the smugglers back to Frank and Joe. The Hardys stood up to face a scarred Mexican agent who was with the police.

"Chavo," Frank said in surprise. "Glad you could make it."

"*Sí,*" replied Chavo. "As you can see, I really am a policeman. We caught all the others on Puerto de Oro, all except these." He swept his arm at Charity and the Director. "Once we find the stolen jewels and cash, the case is, as you say, all wrapped up."

"Mind if we borrow a helicopter and some cops?" Joe said. He held up their cuffed wrists. "And could we get out of these things? There's no key, but the cops have experience with this sort of thing, don't they?"

Chavo went to speak to the police, and a second later came back with an officer, who had Charity in tow. She poked her pin into the locks, and in seconds the handcuffs popped open.

"This lady has something to say to you," Chavo said.

The smile on Charity's face was warm and sincere, without a hint of deceit. "Looks like you won this one, Joe. Maybe next time it'll be my turn again."

"There's not going to be a next time," Joe said. He put the handcuffs on her and handed her over to the policeman. "Don't let her out of your sight, officer. She's tricky."

Dust and sand were whipped around by the wind from the blades of a helicopter as it set down a dozen yards from Chavo and the Hardys. On the helicopter were the markings of the U.S. Border Patrol. "Come," Chavo said. Sprinting, he led the Hardys to the chopper. A door flew open, and a border patrolman reached out to help them inside. There were two other patrolmen on board, as well as the pilot. As the door clicked shut behind them, the helicopter rose twirling into the sky, to fly in ever-widening circles over the desert.

"There's San Diego," Joe exclaimed, spotting the downtown area off in the distance.

"Is that what we're looking for?" Chavo asked.

"No," Frank replied. They sped across the sky, and Frank scoured the roads that led across the desert. One led north and petered out after a mile. Most of the others ran toward San Diego, but there was no sign of a van on any of them. "Head east," he said to the pilot over the pounding of the blades.

On the road to the east, a plume of dust rose. At the tip of the plume was the rent-a-van.

"That's him," Joe said. As the helicopter flew over the van, Chavo opened a footlocker inside the police helicopter and took out several shotguns. He handed one to Frank.

Frank shook his head. "I'd rather not use a gun if I can avoid it."

"Renner won't give us any more trouble," Joe said as he settled in the seat next to the pilot. He snatched a microphone from the dashboard and asked the pilot, "Is there an external loudspeaker on this thing?" The pilot nodded and switched it on.

"You might as well give up, Renner," Joe said into the microphone, and he was thrilled to hear his voice boom back at him from the outside. "You can't get away."

"Good job, Joe," Frank said, his eyes on the road. "He's speeding up."

"Take it down," Chavo ordered with a sigh. He cocked the shotgun. "Get ready."

The chopper set down on the road, blocking it. As the van began backing up, the three border guards charged out of the chopper, firing warning shots into the air.

The van came to a dead stop. Renner stepped out, gun in hand. Spreading his arms wide, he crouched down and dropped the gun to the sand, then stood with his hands up. The border patrolmen rushed him.

"What's the matter?" Joe asked Renner as the police pushed the insurance man to the helicopter. "How come you're not throwing your weight around now?"

Feebly Renner looked at the patrolmen and said, "My name is Elroy Renner. I'm an insurance investigator, and you're interfering with a case. You'll all be in big trouble."

"Save it," Frank said. One by one, he emptied Renner's pockets.

A large sapphire fell from his pants pocket to the sand. Joe crouched to pick it up.

"Well, well," Joe said, holding the Star of

Ishtar up for examination. "I guess this gets Chief Collig off the hook. You stole it all along."

"Get him out of here," Chavo told the patrolmen, and they loaded Renner into the chopper. They watched as it took off.

Turning to the van, Joe said, "I guess we'd better take it back."

"Perhaps . . ." Chavo said in a dreamy voice. His eyes glazed over, and a hungry smile came to his lips. "So much wealth in this van. Split three ways, it could make some people very rich."

"Are you *sure* you're a cop?" Frank asked.

Laughing, Chavo gave a happy-go-lucky shrug. "A man can dream, my friend." He climbed behind the steering wheel of the van. "Do you need a lift anywhere?"

Frank and Joe got in. "How about back to what's left of the plane?"

Chavo shrugged again, and in silence they drove to the west.

The van pulled up beside the charred remains of the plane, near a cluster of policemen who had gathered around the criminals. Joe noticed their agitation. He hopped out of the cab and ran to them, scanning for a face that was missing, feeling his own face flushing with anger.

"Where's the woman?" he shouted. "Where's Charity?"

The police officer Joe had left Charity with turned red with embarrassment, and Joe felt his temper rising. "I can't explain it," the officer said. "I was handcuffed to her one minute, then there was this commotion and I turned away, and the next minute the handcuff was open and she was gone." Seeing Joe's growing rage, he hastily added, "But she can't have gotten far in this desert. As soon as we're in the air, we'll spot her."

"You won't," Joe assured the policeman. He realized Frank was now standing beside him, and exclaimed, "I don't believe it! She got away again." He shook his head, the anger flooding out of him. Somehow there seemed no point in staying mad.

"Look on the bright side," Frank said. "At least this time she went away empty-handed. We'll get her in the next round."

"Oh, no," Joe said as they walked back to Chavo, ready to begin the trip home. "We are never having anything to do with that woman ever again."

Frank nodded his agreement. But deep down, both of them knew that Joe was wrong.

Frank and Joe's next case:

When Bayport is hit by a rash of vicious pranks, the Hardys investigate. They aren't sure the tricks are meant to be funny, especially the mysterious phone tip that leads them to a spooky mansion that happens to be on fire.

After dousing the blaze, the brother detectives find a vital clue. The trail leads them to a bizarre club dedicated to danger. But the pranks may be only a cover for an ultraserious game plan. Soon the young sleuths find themselves playing straight men for a deadly practical joke . . . in *The Deadliest Dare,* Case #30 in The Hardy Boys Casefiles™.

Forthcoming Titles in the
Hardy Boys™ Casefiles Series

Forthcoming Titles in the
Nancy Drew Files™ Series

Simon & Schuster publish a wide range of titles from pre-school books to books for adults.

For up-to-date catalogues, please contact:

International Book Distributors
Campus 400
Maylands Avenue
Hemel Hempstead
Herts
HP2 7EZ

Tel. 0442 882255